THE
CONTRACT
FOR LIFE

THE
CONTRACT
FOR LIFE

Robert Anastas

**Founder and Executive Director of <u>SADD</u>
with KALIA LULOW**

PUBLISHED BY POCKET BOOKS NEW YORK

Another *Original* publication of POCKET BOOKS

The Drug Awareness Test and Indications of Abuse
appear by permission of Drugs and Abuse, Inc.

 POCKET BOOKS, a division of Simon & Schuster, Inc.
1230 Avenue of the Americas, New York, N.Y. 10020

ISBN: 0-671-61874-1

First Pocket Books trade paperback printing June, 1986

10 9 8 7 6 5 4 3 2 1

POCKET and colophon are registered trademarks
of Simon & Schuster, Inc.
SADD and the SADD logo are registered with the United States Patent
and Trademark Office. All rights reserved by S.A.D.D.—Students
Against Driving Drunk, Inc., a Massachusetts non-profit corporation.

Printed in the U.S.A.

To my loving wife, Carol, and my three sons,
Willy, Jeffrey and Mark. Without their
unwavering belief and support my dream
could not have come true.

To all the kids and parents across the
country who have taken the SADD
message to heart, to be there for each
other.

To John and Buddy, to whom SADD is
a living memorial.

Acknowledgments

This book owes an enormous debt to Governor John Volpe, the honorary chairman of SADD, as well as other members of the Board of Directors who, along with the SADD staff, have worked relentlessly since the beginning and who continue to reaffirm that if we dream, *It can be done*. Also, SADD could not have become real, and continue to be a reality, without the generosity of our contributors.

A special thanks to the students at Wayland High School in 1982, and the former governor of Massachusetts, Edward King, whose participation in the first SADD event helped launch SADD nationally.

This book might not have been written without the persistence, encouragement, involvement, commitment and friendship of my literary agent, George Greenfield.

Furthermore, I would like to thank Kalia Lulow for her writing skills and spirited participation in our lives and work and our editor Sydny Weinberg Miner for the fine guidance she provided throughout the writing of the book.

Contents

THE
CONTRACT
FOR LIFE

ONE

As You Sow, So Shall You Reap

We get as much out of life as we put into it. Garbage in, garbage out; quality in, quality out. It's as much work to do a job badly as to do it well, so we all might as well do a good job.
That's what this book is all about.

—Robert Anastas

Introduction

A Will to Live

I have traveled across the country and I have followed death.

Every year our teenagers bury almost 8,000 of their own. They die because of drunk driving: *The number one killer of young people sixteen through twenty.* They don't die in single numbers. They die in groups. They die with two or three friends.

Since 1981, when I founded Students Against Driving Drunk, I have lectured at thousands of high schools after this killer struck. Nine young people died on Long Island, three in Iowa, two in Oregon. In each instance, a week later, I was there. City after city, day after day, the roll call of death seemed endless. These kids weren't from some strange town. They were your neighbors, even your children.

It was a grim reality, and it was a reality I had to face, just as the teenagers had to face the fact that they were burying their own. It was why I introduced the SADD program to more than 3 million teenagers and their parents. It's why I continue to travel hundreds of thousands of miles to all fifty states and Europe. It's why SADD's regional representatives and I spend our days and nights in strange towns and distant airports.

Since 1981, however, a wonderful thing has happened. You, teenagers and parents, began to fight back with enormous passion and power. You said, "We can beat this killer. We can take care of our own. We are our brothers' and sisters', sons' and daughters', mothers' and fathers', keepers!"

These days the roll call of death is shorter. Drinking among teenagers has dropped 10%. The death rate due to drunk driving among teenagers has fallen 33%. Your efforts and mine are working. But we cannot rest until *no* young person is robbed of his or her future by this needless tragedy.

The Contract for Life is the story of troubles with our young people and in our families. But it is also the story of love reclaimed and rekindled.

I have offered my efforts through SADD to atone for my errors as a drug and alcohol counselor who did not know he was blind. And the kids have responded by saying, "We shall show you the way."

The story of the development of SADD—how it began, how my family, friends and students helped get the organization started, and how it has grown—proves that our young people want to and can improve the quality of their lives. And I believe, beyond a shadow of a doubt, that although it is a story born of sadness, it has a joyous ending.

1

** **1** ****

The Saddest Tale

July 4, 1981 was a beautiful, breezy summer's morning. It was a day for celebrating, not only a national holiday but my son Jeffrey's twelfth birthday party, with a cookout on the beach. My other sons, Mark and Willy, were racing around. Surfing gear lay in great piles on the kitchen floor. From one of the bedrooms, a radio played.

Ignoring the din, my wife, Carol, glided through the kitchen routine getting baskets of food ready for the party.

I can hear my voice, full of love and demands. "Where are you going, Mark?" "Willy, what's your schedule?" "Jeffrey, so how's the birthday boy?"

Carol handed me a list of last minute items to get at the

corner store and I left the house filled with that special pride one gets from his treasured family.

While I was gone the phone rang. Just another noise in the raucous kitchen. Carol answered it. (It's funny how the phone always rings when you are too busy to talk.) But even barely listening, she was jolted by the message.

When I walked back into the kitchen Carol and the boys quietly told me the news.

"John's dead."

One of my boys from the hockey team was dead! A kid with pizzaz, and a flash of rebel, a brilliant athlete, a son to me, and a brother to my boys.

John, to whom I lectured every day during the season, "Watch yourself," "Don't drive fast," "Be careful," was dead from a car accident.

At seventeen he was one of the sharpest and brightest hockey players I'd ever coached. As a junior in high school he was being offered scholarships to places like Boston University, Boston College, and Northeastern. Forty thousand dollars' worth of education was in his hands; all he had to do was graduate. But he was an ordinary kid, too. He loved to be part of the group. He loved to have a lot of fun. Now the fun, the scholarships, the future were gone. Gone because he wanted to preserve his image; he thought he could not ask for a ride home. He thought he could challenge death and win.

Let me give you the scenario:

John had gone to a party. At eleven o'clock at night he looked at his watch and said, "Oh my, I have to be home now." What did he do? He did what most kids would do: He drove as fast as he could to get home. He lost control of the car. He hit a tree. And he died.

Standing in my kitchen with Carol and my own sons I felt completely distraught. I knew the facts but nothing made sense. I craved an explanation, something that would answer the question, Why?

I talked to his friends and his parents. At the wake, two days later, I watched a stream of girls in white dresses lay red roses on his coffin. I felt like saying, "Take your red roses, and leave. This is not the time to help John. We can cry all day. He is not coming back."

His teammates and other athletes poured through the funeral home. Big, powerful kids, crying hysterically. I watched one of those boys walk up to his coffin and say, "What the hell are you doing dying on me?"

"Why? Why? Why?" the kids asked me.

I simply said, "Why not? If you challenge death you are going to lose."

When I was alone I raged. I stormed. I protested to the gods. And I fought the slowly creeping feeling that I had failed this kid as surely as he had failed himself.

Four days after we had tamped down the loose black soil over John's grave, the damn phone rang again. Two phone calls within a week. This time a nineteen-year-old boy, Buddy, who had been on my hockey team, was driving home from the beach with a friend. The car flipped over. The boys both suffered head injuries. Buddy was in a coma. His friend, who is alive today and still struggles with the physical repercussions of the accident, was severely injured.

Buddy had been a real star; now he was without light. I watched him die for three days. I sat vigil with his friends, praying that he'd come out of the coma.

I watched the kids come to his bedside, yelling in his ear, "Wake up." I saw the girls crying. On the third day after the accident the doctor told us, "Medically he's dead. If you see an eyelash move, anything, I don't care what, let me know." That was when one of Buddy's friends, a young girl, pulled a pin out of her purse and stuck it in his leg. Nothing. She stuck him again. Nothing. She put the pin back in her purse and walked away.

We sat as the doctor pulled the plug.

One more senseless tragedy. One more funeral. Our ordinary family, our ordinary small town, was experiencing extraordinary grief. We were not alone: Thousands and thousands of times a year, teenagers lost their friends; mothers and fathers lost their children. John and Buddy were snatched from our lives by the same fate that was stealing young lives around the country.

I was barely able to respond to the world around me. My mind was filled with the horrible chant . . . *living . . . dying . . . so young . . . living . . . dying . . . so young. . . .*

These were the saddest moments of my life.

** **2** **

Death and Determination

There comes a time in every life when we are each forced to examine the results of our life. At that moment, despite our desire to feel satisfied, we each clearly see our mistakes. It is then we have a choice: to hide from ourselves or face our flaws. No one ever enjoys that moment, but it is a welcome one nonetheless, for it is the time when we can finally right our wrongs. That is what happened to me after the two boys died. For I saw for the first time what I could do personally to stop kids from dying.

Summer 1981 wound down. The sticky heat of the end of August brought with it the familiar sounds of school: players crowding the locker room, listening to coaches' speeches, slamming themselves against the blocking forms, preparing—always hopeful—for the battles they would face during the school year.

My own sons were full of life. Each one was preparing to confront a new set of demands from their ever-expanding world. Carol was still emotionally battered by the deaths of "our" boys, but she kept her pain to herself. I was numb. Those around me saw my sadness and anger, but I was oblivious to my own feelings.

Late at night, when the rush of the day had passed, we would talk about anything but what was really on our minds. The strain was sharp; we had always met life's challenges head on.

Mark now tells me that during those days everyone in the house seemed different. He was not able to articulate what he saw and felt but he knew something had changed drastically. Jeffrey puts it more forcefully: "At first the house was quiet; no one dared to say anything for fear of upsetting someone. As time went by, the oppressive mood sunk in deeper and deeper."

Old Lectures, Old Mistakes

I had been involved in health education and counseling for twenty years. I had coached hockey and football for ten years. I had spent most of my life trying to help kids grow into strong, capable individuals. In 1971, I was the Massachusetts State Teacher of the Year, and won a National Merit Award in Education for my work in alcohol and drug education. I moved on to a position as health administrator for the Wayland school system. That fall, after the two boys died, I couldn't stand being out of the classroom. So I set up a new health program at Wayland for sophomores, focusing on alcohol and drug education. The kids were taken out of their regular Physical Education class on a rotating basis. Buzzy Bowers, the physical education director, and Dr. Charles Goff, the principal, gave me their complete support. The program consumed all my attention.

Every class was typically unique, a glorious hodgepodge of kids from all different backgrounds, all different races, with different sets of personal problems and abilities. Yet each of their faces, all turned towards me, held a look of hope.

The first week I launched into my standard rap. Statistics about alcohol and drugs covered the blackboard. I forced the kids to memorize the list of physical, emotional and community horrors that drugs create. I marched pictures of traffic accidents in front of their eyes.

There was not a student who was unaware of the deaths of John and Buddy. Wayland is a small school, in a town that cares about its children. These kids had older brothers and sisters who were classmates of the dead boys. They had cheered them on during the hockey season. They had looked up to them, and now they knew that they were dead.

They also knew that I was a wreck. I have never been good at disguising what I'm feeling. Except in this instance, I hid it from myself.

The first week, some of my anger and sadness broke through the dry statistics in every class. By Friday I started pacing back and forth, lapsing into silences. The kids watched quietly.

As the bell rang to signal the end of class I turned and shouted at their backs, "This is not working. This is stupid."

They froze, but none of them contradicted me. They would have if they thought I was wrong.

"John and Buddy knew everything I'm teaching you," I shouted. "They knew. And they died."

All weekend I puzzled over my explosion. I told Carol about it and she tried to make me understand that it was because I still felt the pain so sharply. I argued. I raged.

Monday came. The kids sat in their rows of seats looking at me. Wondering, no doubt, what Mr. A. was going to do today.

"Kids," I started without knowing where I was going, "kids, you are responsible for the boys dying. Yes, you. Don't look at me.

"Think about it. You drive a car drunk, and die. I don't. You get in a car with your friends after they've been drinking. I don't. You go to athletic events and then celebrate with a couple of beers. We adults aren't there; you know who's been drinking. I don't.

23

"You're out there. I'm not. Your parents aren't. Your teachers aren't. You have made choices that keep me, and your parents, out of your private lives but you haven't got enough sense to take responsibility for yourselves.

"You have to police yourselves. If you have the information about drinking and driving then the solution lies with you. To find a solution you have to know what the problem is. If the only problem is drunk driving, then don't drink, or don't get into a car drunk or with someone else who's drunk. But there must be bigger, less obvious problems, otherwise it wouldn't be so hard to find a solution. Those problems are hidden from me, and they seem to be hidden from you, too."

I hammered at them for the whole hour, my throat tightening with every word. I was red and shaking. The kids didn't move a muscle.

"I'm telling you *I don't know how to do this*. I need your help. What I have been doing has failed."

The class ended in a tense silence. A few kids carefully asked, "Are you okay?"

As the bell rang they seemed reluctant to rush off to their next class. I remember two students, in particular, who stayed a few extra minutes. Clutching their notebooks, they stared at the floor, and offered encouragement. "We'll do something to figure this out, Mr. A."

But I was not feeling encouraged. I hadn't accomplished my job.

I questioned myself as a person, an educator. I questioned the whole educational system, its relationship to the parents and their kids.

I admitted I didn't know the kids—not their hearts, not where they lived their secret teenage lives, not where they faced death alone. I finally saw how isolated we were from one another. We had not been working together. We had not been communicating. The results were that we felt terrible loneliness, confusion and fear, but we pretended that everything was great. We educators pretended we were as wise as Solomon. The parents offered the kids the material comforts and pretended it took the place of emotional security. The kids pretended they were smart and savvy and could handle themselves. We were all lying to each other and to ourselves. We had formed a community of the blind and the false. I felt sick from the realization and hopeful from facing the truth.

By Wednesday my desperation was at its peak. When the kids trooped into the room I made them pull their chairs into a semicircle so we could each look at one another. I sat on the end; I didn't feel like I had the right to make myself the center of the group or be the leader. Then I heard the sound of Lou, the janitor, rolling his trash cart down the hall. It was a big slung canvas bin on hard black rubber wheels. Every revolution of the wheels echoed off the marble floor and created a rhythm that seemed to demand some action.

Like a man possessed, I swept through the class picking up all the books, papers, and literature that I used to teach the kids, great armfuls of empty words and useless advice. As Lou approached the door to my classroom I walked out to meet him and threw every last piece of material into the trash bin.

He never broke stride. He simply nodded and carried the useless texts away.

"We are going to stop this cycle of drinking and driving and dying," I declared when I came back into the room. "I don't know how but we are going to do it."

The kids smiled. One or two applauded. They laughed with relief that I wasn't mad at them.

The first day that the kids and I began working together I told them the story of my life, about my parents, about college. I wanted them to know that I was like them. I had a history and a complex family background. If I was willing to trust them with my personal feelings and thoughts, then, perhaps, I would earn the right to be trusted with theirs.

"Look," I promised them, "I'll fight anyone you want. You just have to give me the inspiration and the information I need to do it. I need your advice and your help.

They responded with more questions: "What do we do?" "How can we make a difference?"

On the board I wrote:

DEATH   LIFE

"Here are your choices. We need to figure out how to get death away from you. It is possible. It's in your control. *You* have the power of life; you don't have to choose to die from drinking and driving. And since drunk driving is the number one killer of kids your age, if you turn it aside you have chosen life."

The idea that they had power, that they could make a difference, filled the room with an electricity. We had started our journey together. None of us knew just how far it would take us, but we knew that something had changed.

The kids did a lot of talking. They described their parties. They told about all the times they had been in cars with someone who was drunk. They admitted their fears. They poured out their confusions about dealing with all the pressures they felt. Slowly they noticed that they all felt it—and they all wanted to get out of the pressure situation where they couldn't refuse to drink, or drink and drive.

In the first weeks we all spoke at once. Everyone had questions; no one had answers. We hadn't yet been able to pinpoint the problems that made the kids victims.

When I sat with Carol at night and discussed the classes, I'd cry. I was searching for some key to understanding why our kids were dying needlessly.

At three o'clock one morning, I leapt out of bed, turned on the light and declared, "I've figured something out.

"The kids are in a death box, just like John and Buddy's coffin. The walls of the coffin are the hidden pressures that make it hard to solve the problem of drinking, and drinking and driving.

"One wall of the death box is created by the kids' desire to preserve their parents' perfect image of them. How can a seventeen-year-old call up and say, 'I've fouled up. I have been drinking and I can't drive'? It would hurt his mother or enrage his father. So he gets into his car and takes a chance, and sometimes, he kills himself.

"The second wall of the death box is peer pressure. Kids feel trapped by the pressure to go along with what they think is socially acceptable drinking and drug use. They don't understand how negative peer pressure can be broken and positive peer pressure can take its place.

"The third wall is innocence and ignorance. Kids don't understand their own mortality; they don't know they can die. They don't know that when you're dead at seventeen, you're dead. So they challenge death in order to preserve their parents' image of them and to be accepted by their peers, and they die.

"The last wall, and it's a beauty, is built by lack of communication. Parents don't talk to their kids. Kids don't tell their parents what they do or feel or fear. Growing up has become a process of systematically cutting themselves off from those who should be closest to them—their family.

"Those four walls seal the fate of our kids. We have to tear them down. We must build respect and trust in the family so that when someone needs help they can ask for it, and get it. We must be stronger parents—and stronger children."

Carol was sitting up in bed with a gleeful, electrified look on her face; she knew that she was watching the beginnings of a powerful new idea. We talked for hours. From the very first Carol has understood, sometimes before I did, what the issues were. She offered suggestions, probed, and cried. By dawn we fell into a peaceful, short sleep.

Creating a New Program

During the 1981–82 school year the kids and I worked together in class, after school, with the principal and the other teachers, to find the best way to change patterns of drug and alcohol abuse. We stewed, fumed, searched for the ideas and methods to get across the message:

"My love for you and your love for me is enough to keep you from ever foolishly risking your life."

I was constantly hit by the realization that they had been waiting, silently, for someone to help them.

27

"Why didn't you ever tell me that all my teaching wasn't working?" I asked my student Carl Olsen, who became the Wayland SADD Chapter's first president.

"Because you never asked," I recall was his simple response.

Well, we were asking now, and the kids were giving us adults answers we couldn't have imagined.

They were telling us what they wanted to know. We worked with them to arrange programs, asking them for their input— and listening.

I organized a series of guest speakers to come in and answer the kids' questions. We had a steady stream of presentations from people like Walter DeVoe of the Alcohol Beverage Commission and Massachusetts state trooper Ken Carew.

Carew told of the horrors he'd seen. He shared his feelings, not just the facts. He brought in gruesome films that made the kids begin to understand that their youth was no protection against death. It is hard for teenagers to grasp the possibility of their mortality. That is one reason they challenge death. They don't understand that if they are dead at seventeen, they will miss the wonders their future can hold. He wasn't afraid to tell the classes how bad he felt, how scared he was. He was the first law enforcement official the kids ever knew as a person.

Slowly, through luck and hard work, we were breaking down the barriers between the school, parents, law enforcement and the kids.

I wanted some kind of ongoing organization, but none of us knew what it might be.

Hall of Mirrors

All through that school year, well before we formalized SADD, I had begun to test out the emerging concepts on my colleagues, parents, and other concerned leaders in the drug and alcohol field.

For years I had been participating in national lecture tours and professional meetings and I had forged friendships with a wide variety of people involved with drug and alcohol abuse. Many of us worked with the National Commission for the Prevention of Alcoholism and Drug Dependence, of which I am currently a board member.

Among those who I knew, loved, and worked with were Alan Cohen of the Pacific Institute, a research scholar in the field, and William Plymat, founder of Preferred Risk Insurance and cofounder of one of the strongest pro-abstinence groups in the country, the American Council on Alcohol Problems (ACAP). We were all united by our determination to break the tragic cycle of illegal drug and alcohol use and abuse by young people, but we each came to the issue from very different perspectives.

March of 1982 was the annual meeting of the National Commission in Orlando, Florida. Many of us were scheduled to speak to the 150 or so colleagues who had assembled there. My talk was supposed to be on the same old teaching techniques we educators had been using to instruct our students on prevention of drug and alcohol use.

I was still in an intensely emotional state, angry at the boys' deaths and haunted by the spectre of failure that touched every educational program I had conducted over the past twenty years.

As the meeting started I glanced around the auditorium. No one was doing anything any differently than they had done the year before. Or than they would do next year.

Then it was my turn to talk. I had no idea what was going to come out of my mouth; I simply started speaking.

"We are all still talking about the same old teaching techniques we have used for years," I shouted. "We are telling each other the same old facts about cirrhosis of the liver, the death of brain cells from drugs and alcohol, the biological effects of substance abuse. We've known these facts for years. We are boring ourselves, and we go back to our classrooms and bore our students. You'd think we'd have learned by now. These facts are not what we need to keep our kids healthy and alive. We need a whole new approach.

"Not once in this program have we ever given up a moment of our time to hear from the kids we are supposed to be helping. The kids are the ones who have the experience and the insight to help us forge solutions.

"I don't know about you but I have a problem. I used to be sold on me, the expert, but I have finally been confronted with reality and it doesn't make me happy about myself or our profession. Our kids are killing themselves. *We* have done nothing to stop that. You know why. Because we can't. Only the kids can kill themselves and only they can save themselves. *We* can't lecture them and hope to have any effect. You don't shout swimming instructions to a drowning child! You don't stand on the shore and say, 'Hey, you should have learned to swim before you jumped in the pool. Well now, as you're taking in water, let's review the techniques for the Australian crawl!' If you want to have any effect at all you help the kids realize that they must learn to swim *before* they get in the water.

"Sure, sometimes we need to jump in and drag them to shore if they are drowning. But we'd all be a lot happier if a lot fewer of them found themselves in peril of drowning at all!

"We have never asked the kids to *do* anything before; we let them be passive recipients of our wise words, but we don't ask them to act. *And* we don't ask them for their opinions about how we should act to help them the most.

"We can say *no* to death by letting the kids take charge. My new program is designed to do that. It is run by the kids, for the kids. We are coworkers with them, but we do the work *they* tell us needs to be done.

"These kids don't have to die. They can solve their problems. They don't have to listen to our useless words anymore, and we don't either.

"This assembly, my friends, is a Hall of Mirrors. We sit and stare at our own reflection of imagined brilliance, full of self-congratulation. We think we are speaking to the world, even saving the world, but we are only talking to ourselves."

The dead silence that followed my explosion continued for

several minutes. I was exhausted. When I collected myself I said, more quietly, "I will be available to talk to you and provide you with written material if you are interested. This can be one of the most powerful life-affirming movements ever started."

From that moment on I began to formalize the SADD concept and work on ways to make it a self-sufficient program. I was desperate to find a way to launch the still unnamed SADD.

Back at Wayland, I gathered fifteen of the most committed students from my health class and started meeting with them regularly. Our goal was to come up with the issues and ideas we thought would help break down the walls of the death box, and reveal how the reality of death had been hidden from them.

The first issue we addressed was *negative peer pressure*. We all remember it; it's part of adolescence, like puberty and pimples. It is the incredibly heavy feeling that we have to fit in, be accepted, go along with the crowd.

Teenagers are neither children nor adults. They have lost the external security of being able to say, "My mommy won't let me," and they do not yet have the internal strength of character to say, "I won't let myself."

Sitting in a quiet classroom after school hours, the kids and I found the time and the need to explore the problem. I asked them: "How can you get to the point where you are comfortable enough with yourself to be able to say, 'I don't want to drink tonight'? How can you say to your girl friend, 'I have my dad's car. I'm not drinking. I'm not going to do anything I don't want to do'? How can your girl friend say, 'You've been drinking. I'm not riding home with you. I'm calling my parents for a ride for both of us'? And how can you all feel comfortable enough to say to a friend, 'You've been drinking too much. That's it. Grow up. Knock it off. We don't want to lose you'?"

The kids explained the difficulties. They said, "We aren't about to interfere." "We'd get laughed at." "My date would leave me." "I'd be embarrassed."

"I'm here," I told them, "to help each of you feel comfortable and intimate with your peers. You have got to open up enough to tell each other how you think and feel. You've cut out your family and your teachers. At least open up to your classmates!"

High schools are often very divided camps consisting of social groups and cliques that have a lot of power; kids from one group don't talk to or show any care for kids in another group. But in my health classes and in the smaller groups, kids from all the groups spent time together, getting to feel close to one another. The discussions of peer pressure led to discussions about the different social groups. And as a result they all recognized a truth: Underneath all the differences in dress, or hair styles, or attitudes, each of the kids felt very similarly about peer pressure.

They each admitted they felt they had to go along with attitudes and behavior they didn't like. They each wished they were free from peer pressure. When they discovered this they were relieved; they no longer felt isolated or threatened by the pressures. The kids decided they could form a new group—one that exerted pressure to act responsibly; it was their first chance to develop a sense of communal power.

In the classroom the students began to build bridges of care between their divided cliques. They began to see each other as individuals. Kids who never spoke to one another, who certainly would never have cared if the other person drank, were taking the time to talk to one another, to reach out and say, "Don't drink. Don't drink and drive. I care about you and I want you to care about me."

Once we had explored all the hidden terrors of peer pressure, the kids began to talk about the problems they had with their parents. The first one they admitted was the struggle to keep their parents' idealized image of them intact. Every one of the kids, from the achievers through the silent middle to the rebels, all felt they could not express their individuality because it clashed with their parents' expectations of them.

I asked the kids, "What can parents and teachers do to help

you feel better about yourselves, so you don't hide your individual opinions and feelings?" And they all answered: "Stop shoveling your expectations on us!"

Look at it from the kids' point of view:

Parents have a very well-developed set of expectations for teenagers, stated or unstated. The kids know that their elders want them to make choices that fit those expectations, even if they are the wrong choices for the child. (You can see it in college selections all the time, when parents say, My son is definitely a Yale man! The kid knows he's made for Beloit College!)

Such expectations, piled one on top of another, make a teenager who is struggling to find self-definition cry out, "Am I really an individual or simply a jumble of what my parents want me to be? Who am I and where am I going?"

The kids have trouble with our unreasonable expectations, but this doesn't mean we are useless or should shut up and go away. Kids need our authority, discipline and guidance. They need us in order to become the best they can be. We can participate in the formation of their choices if we listen to their point of view and help them make the best selection from the alternatives they have available. We are not giving up a parental authority by helping them develop individual, evaluating minds; we are using our authority to its best effect.

The kids were telling me more than I ever learned from lecturing to them! They were telling me they were ready to take reasonable responsibility for their lives—and ready to work with us adults in the process.

As the school year progressed I began to feel better. At night when I'd come home to my family I was calmer, less tormented. I spent my days surrounded by the blossoming hope and love of the students at school. My own feelings of hope and love reemerged.

** 3 **

The Joy of SADD

> I was learning; the kids were teaching me every day. I finally understood that if we keep preaching *at* them, it is not going to make the problem of drinking, and drinking and driving go away. For twenty-two years I talked *at* kids about drinking. Now the kids were going to act to help each other.

By early 1982 we had talked enough. I was determined to stop the death of our children—one an hour, eight or nine thousand a year—from drunk driving. It was time to formalize an organization at Wayland High School. I called it Students Against Driving Drunk. That was the point.

In the beginning days of SADD a small percentage of people mistakenly thought that SADD was not as concerned with the issue of teenage drinking as it was with teenage drinking and driving. This was not true. I wanted our kids home, *alive,* so we could tackle the problems of teenage drinking.

For years, educators and counselors have been searching for the best way to help kids stop alcohol and drug use, but we didn't understand how eager the kids were to help themselves solve the problem. SADD's message is one that kids are enthusiastic about. It is straightforward, not preachy, and it has immediate, beneficial effects on their lives.

Adults and professionals in the drug and alcohol field who disapprove of SADD have simply not looked at what SADD's far-reaching effects are.

Larry Rotta, a SADD Michigan representative, states that the transition from getting kids to stop kids from using alcohol and driving, to getting kids to stop kids from using alcohol and drugs is a short step. "The SADD kids make the move spontaneously," he explains. "The proof is in the type of presentations and projects they take to the younger kids. The whole message is, 'Don't drink or do drugs at all.' "

The 3.3 million teenage alcoholics in this country will not disappear if we simply ignore them. Cocaine use among teenagers, which has tripled, will not go away by wishing. We are faced with realities we must address. Drug and alcohol abuse is a disease. SADD is an effective vaccine that helps keep this disease from killing our children. A program that gains loyalty and support among kids and that brings parents and kids together through better communication—a program called SADD—can only help the kids to better help themselves.

By the end of the spring semester of 1982, just six months after we formed the organization, we had begun to encounter the first objections to SADD's approach to the problem of drinking and driving, but the kids were determined to see SADD flourish, because they were determined to have a good future for themselves and their friends. All 250 students in Wayland's sophomore class had been through my health program. Each of them made a major contribution to the new, well-defined goals and principles of the organization.

WHAT IS SADD?

The basic organization, that was formed by the hard work of the Wayland kids, myself and the school, is run by kids, for kids. It is designed to keep them alive by eliminating their number one killer: drunk driving. Its ultimate goal is to get kids off drugs and booze.

SADD has a far-reaching effect on the lives of the students and parents who participate in it. They learn how to work together to improve their relationships in all areas of their lives.

The emotional force behind the SADD message is: Let's have love and trust. The techniques we use are open communication and a willingness to recognize, identify and deal with reality.

The results are better management of all family problems concerning drugs, sexual behavior, academic excellence and communication.

When a family joins together to work for SADD they begin to learn about each other. There are a lot of surprises. While the kids are opening up communication between themselves to counteract negative peer pressure, their families must work to overcome their lack of communication, too. When this process begins, very often the first topic of discussion centers around the fact that kids have a big problem because *they want to make their parents happy!*

That's right. Kids want to make their parents happy.

I know that doesn't sound like a problem. "Dear God," parents say. "If they would only do that!" But listen to the subtext.

Your kids have a whole life that is secret from you. When they were young children you were their universe, their main support system. You provided for them; they depended on you. Slowly, as they grew older, they moved away. They began to depend on their peers. They began to feel that you were inaccessible. They kept secrets. They closed you out of their intimate world.

To some extent this is as it should be. Children must enter the world on their own terms. But what happens is that they cut themselves off from their greatest source of love and advice: the family. And in its place they look to other kids, as uncertain about life as they are, for guidance and approval.

You still want to believe that they are the wonderful, pure

children you knew. You want to believe that the hardships of life will somehow pass them by. You hope they don't have to deal with drugs and alcohol or sexual pressures, and so you approach them with an attitude that says: "You're fine, aren't you, honey?"

In order for them to tell you that you are mistaken, they have to be willing at fifteen or sixteen or nineteen to say, "No, I'm not fine. No, I'm not the wonderful child you once knew. No, I'm not perfect."

That's asking a lot of any kid. That's even asking a lot of an adult. Imagine how you'd feel in the same situation.

So instead the kids decide that they'll keep you happy. They won't destroy your pretty vision of them and their world, and when you ask them how they are they say, "Great," and go off by themselves to try to figure out how to handle whatever pressures they feel.

When they find themselves in a group where there is drinking or drugs or where they feel pressure to act in ways they'd rather not, they can't come home and say, "Hey Dad, what should I do?" They can't admit out loud to you that they have come in contact with situations that you wouldn't approve of.

Because our kids want to make us happy they end up hurting themselves and us! It is a tragedy of love, not hate. But the results are tragic nonetheless.

We are destroying ourselves in the name of keeping the family happy.

Lack of communication is one of the walls of the Death Box that parents must and can help their children break down. It's not easy.

In the age of mass media there seems to be a word shortage. The TV blares; the stereo screams; magazines, newspapers, books, fill our heads with other people's words. But where are our own words? Parents live under enormous social and economic pressures. They are tired and harassed. Kids, fearing conflicts and confrontation, retreat. We rarely spend an hour a day together with no sound but those of our own voices.

Our kids get further and further away from us. Think of all

the things that your kids keep to themselves: for example, concerns about sex, drugs, boy-girl relationships.

Every day they are concerned about one or more of those topics. They take their worries to bed each night and think, "Oh my, I'll never get through tomorrow." The worries build up in them and cause heartaches, fear and turmoil. Your kids walk through the house, past you, and out the door carrying these fears.

Adolescent problems are not always trivial. Our kids face real life crises, and far too often they face them alone, without our guidance or help. Let me give you an example. I talked to a girl recently who came up to me after an assembly and said, "You know something, Mr. A., I was going to kill myself, because I thought I was pregnant and it was driving me crazy. But I talked to someone and she helped me through that bad time. Now that I know that I'm not pregnant I feel okay. But it was hard, because I didn't know what to do. I didn't know where to go, who to see, or who to talk to."

There is a privacy circle that kids live in every day, the circle that contains all their intimate thoughts. When they want to discuss their private world, whom do they turn to? They go to the circle of people around them who are known as *intimates*. And who are the intimate people in a teenager's life, Mom and Dad? Can your teenager come home and say, "Daddy, I want you to sit down right now, put the paper down, put the coffee aside. I want to talk to you about a sexual concern I have"? Can your teenager come home tonight and say, "Mommy, I've got a real problem. I want to tell you about it"? Or will you respond, "Do the dishes. What do you want to tell me about that for?"

Where are Mom and Dad in their children's circle of privacy? Are they right there, next to them? They should be. Kids need them. No matter what reasons there are for being distant from your children, the results are still the same. The kids are forced to look outside the intimate family circle for communication. And do you know where they go? To their friends.

Their friends may be great kids, but they are kids with many of the same confusions and needs as your child. Do you know which friends they look to for advice and guidance? Mom and Dad often have no idea. We often force our kids to hide their friends from us because they know we would not approve of them, and as a result of this parents don't ever get a clear idea of the influences that their children's friends have on them. The children move further and further away from the intimate circle where the parents should be the primary source of communication and love.

Outside a child's circle of friends are the circle of acquaintances and strangers. If you, as a parent, don't know what's going on with your kids' friends, you'll probably never know what they encounter in their world outside that, and then one day it becomes clear that you are now an acquaintance or even a stranger yourself! How did it happen? Now you must go back and reclaim that old closeness; but you can't have it exactly as it was. You will only become intimate with your children by facing the complex problems in their world with them.

In my family we have monthly meetings. It may not be spontaneous, but it works. We all assemble around the kitchen table and stare into each other's eyes and mumble out our problems. Carol and I take the lead by starting off the questions. "How have you been getting along with your brothers, Mark?" "What's happening with your history teacher, Jeffrey?" "Do you think your curfew hours are fair, Willy?" Any question will do to break the ice.

The rules are as follows:
1. No one gets to interrupt.
2. Everyone gets to say *anything* they want.
3. No one gets yelled at for what they say.

Believe me it's hard. Sometimes I think the top of my head is going to blow off. The kids don't spare me or Carol; they don't spare each other. This is not something we do for our egos; we do it to hold the family together and make it closer. The result is that Carol and I have had to learn to be grownups too! The temporary pains of small shared truths are so much less than the pains of hidden resentments that we all have learned to take it gladly.

If you haven't talked to your kids lately, try it. The first few sessions may consist mostly of silences; the kids may not come across. But after a number of sessions everyone will begin to trust the process, and you'll find that spontaneous sharing outside the meeting increases, too.

Remember: The goal is to keep your kids from ever being in a situation where their lives are in danger and they can't ask you for help. You want them to live. They want to live. It's that simple, and that serious. So sit down and talk.

The Contract for Life

SADD starts with the premise that we must believe in our children and we want to keep our kids alive. Once they are home, safe and sound, we can address the problems facing them.

To get to the point where our kids can trust us enough to get home alive, and where we can trust them enough to let them admit their mistakes, we need to make a public declaration of our good will.

That's where the Contract for Life comes in.

This contract is a way for us to say, out loud, to each other: I care and I will help you, because my love for you and your love for me is strong enough to overcome any obstacle that makes you challenge death.

The Contract (see page 115) is a formal written agreement signed by a high school student and his or her parents. It acknowledges potential problems and the family's desire to face and manage them. The Contract for Life functions in four important ways:

1. It helps your children to stay out of life-threatening situations when they may feel pressure to be a passenger in a car with someone (adult or peer) who has been drinking.

2. It helps your children avoid being in a life-threatening

situation when they may have had something to drink and are the ones who are driving.

3. It offers your children the assurance that you, too, will avoid placing yourself in a drunk-driving situation.

4. It offers your children the assurance that you will not be a passenger in a car when the driver has been drinking.

The number of innocent passengers who are killed while riding with drunk drivers is enormous. The number of sober responsible drivers who are hit and killed by another car, driven by a drunk driver, is enormous. The Contract for Life is a vital link in the chain of serious efforts by many groups across the country to avoid any of these tragic incidents.

The Contract offers the kids the chance to trust us with their problems, and it asks us to acknowledge that we have problems too. We can't ask our kids to be responsible people and not be equally responsible ourselves.

Now, you may think that such a piece of paper doesn't really mean anything, but Bill Hoenig, California State Superintendent of Schools, who signed the Contract with his son Michael, puts it this way: "There is something special and very emotional about acting together with your child. It really does make you feel good, and it's a chance to share something together."

In families with good parent-child communication the discussion and signing of the Contract is a chance to affirm your commitment to each other. In families with difficult parent-child communication, it is a strong first step to opening the channels of concern. In all families, it offers parents a forum for their concerns and a chance to express their authority and ideas about discipline. The Contract lets the kids express their fears, explain their world and appreciate that their parents' authority comes from love and understanding.

SADD Is Launched

The kids and I had poked and prodded each other until we had teased out the heart and soul of SADD. Our discussions had uncovered the basic problems that all kids, parents, teachers and communities had to confront. Now that we had a solid basis, and the whole school and community were supportive of our aims, it was time to go public!

Fifty kids decided to launch a Prom SADD Week campaign. It would offer alcohol-free pre-prom dinners and supervised post-prom parties and breakfasts, so the students had alternatives to the traditional round of drinking parties that accompany many proms. And it would spread the SADD message all over town.

The kids needed funds, however. So they knocked on local shop keepers' doors; they talked to their parents and their parents employers; they got financial support from retailers, service companies and industry. And they did it simply by asking, straightforwardly, for what they needed.

As a result, they had funds for supplies, paint, balloons, fliers and all the paraphernalia they needed to make SADD Week and the Prom Project effective.

The kids were unbelievably enthusiastic and tough; they wanted to refuse admission to the Prom to any student who had not returned a signed Contract. That idea was vetoed, but their spirit of determination was unquenchable.

Late one Thursday afternoon, as the warm May sunlight cut through the clouds and filled the classroom with the touch of hope that each spring brings, one student said, "Let's get the governor here to launch SADD Week!"

The rest of the kids chuckled. "Right, and let's get the Pope and Mick Jagger, too!"

It sounded right to me. I didn't have any notion of how to make it happen, but it was worth trying. I said, "Remember our motto: *If you can dream, it can be done.* So let's get the governor."

The organizing committee set out to wade through the umpteen levels of bureaucracy surrounding the governor of Massachusetts, Governor Edward King. They finally got close to him, but not close enough for him to actually know, personally, about the project. His support staff responded. They said, "No."

I was furious. The kids had put their hearts and their minds to this; I wasn't going to have them turned down. So I called up the governor's office and said, "Look. You don't know me, but my kids asked Governor King to attend their rally against drunk driving. If he doesn't want to be the honorary chairperson for our organization, Students Against Driving Drunk, and doesn't feel it's important to save kids' lives, we feel sorry for all of you."

The next day the kids got the governor's personal acceptance. We had gotten through to him, and once he heard about SADD Week, his support and enthusiasm were boundless. He was, and continued to be, one of our earliest and most important friends.

So we had the governor. It was the good news and the bad news. We had created something we were not quite prepared for. We didn't have a program scheduled. We didn't know how to work with the press and the media. We didn't have any idea that Wayland SADD week would become the focus of every evening news report across the state.

The kids and I blitzed the state. By the time the governor's helicopter landed on the Wayland football field there were twenty-five dignitaries, from senators and representatives to health care professionals and law enforcement officials, standing on the speaking platform. Meanwhile, the town of Wayland was filled with television crews from around the state.

The kids had seized power. The world was listening. They had never felt more joyous.

Governor King gave a speech and afterwards the kids released 1,000 balloons with the SADD logo on them; they floated on the winds of change. The SADD message swept across the countryside. By the end of the next week, requests for information on SADD were pouring into Wayland High from as far away as California.

We woke up the kids across the country and we had to respond. I had promised the kids that I would be their spokesperson. What a contract we had all made!

TWO

On a Shoestring, in a Shoebox

Everything changed when Bob stopped teaching and started SADD. We didn't know where the money to run SADD was going to come from or how we would get by, but Bob would not let lack of money defeat him. We believed in his belief. It was a family commitment.

When it started, I kept track of everything in a shoebox. Bob was gone all the time. The phone never stopped ringing; the house was in an uproar. I had to learn to do so many new things myself. It was hard. But we all had loved the two boys who died. We weren't going to be defeated just because life had to be lived on a shoestring or the organization had to be run out of a shoebox!

—Carol Anastas

** 4 **

A Family Just Like Yours

I struggled just as you do. I've lived through the results of my life, lived with good intentions and some bad effects. I made two major—I mean *major*—mistakes, and what I've learned is that it is easy to stop foolish self-destruction. I hope my mistakes will help you avoid your own.

We had a secure life, planned out, certain, but I was driven to abandon it.

For weeks in the spring of 1982 I talked to Dr. Charles Goff, the principal of Wayland High School, my brothers, Phillip and George, and my family about quitting teaching to run SADD on a full-time basis. I barely slept at night. I hardly let Carol sleep.

Looking back on the hardships my family and I endured during the first year, I struggle to find the answer to why I started SADD. You know the tragedies that triggered my actions. But as I said, even they are not explanation enough, for they were not unique to me. They were repeated 8,000 times a year. I was no more prepared to take on the task than any other broken-hearted parent. I was just an ordinary man who suddenly found himself galvanized by personal, private passion.

The best I can conclude is that I have done it because I was determined. Any of you could have done it just as well. To me, my story proves that each of us can make a difference. If I did, we all can, if we believe in ourselves.

That's why I want to tell my story.

Hudson, Massachusetts, where I grew up from 1934 to 1952 was a small, hard-working town filled with Italians, Portuguese, Albanians, Greeks, Irish and countless others who had come to this country to find a better life.

Parents worked long hours in shoe factories and textile mills; their children often worked right alongside them. When there was not regular employment, people relied on small hustles and clever schemes. They got by.

All of us kids carried the dreams of our parents in our hearts (and sometimes on our backs). We knew that the sacrifices they made were so that we could have a better life than they had.

My own family was far from the harmonious household that I'd wish for any kid. My old man was tough. He could barely read or write. He ran saloons, did petty hustling, worked in the shoe factory. He scared us half to death.

But that was only one side of his character. He also told us we could do anything if we worked for it. Since he couldn't make life easy for us, we had no choice but to take responsibility for ourselves at an early age.

When I was a freshman in high school he said to me, "Kid, if you want to go to college you're going to have to get an athletic scholarship. I can't help. I don't have the money."

I knew then, at fourteen, that the rest of my life depended on how I played football and hockey at little Hudson High.

That's pressure.

Every step was a battle. I couldn't be just another ball player; I had to be the best. And I came damn close. I put in extra hours of practice every day. It paid off; I learned what it takes to excel. I ran when others walked. I slept when others partied. I worked when others played. I became all-state in hockey and football. I got my scholarship. I was able to attend American International College in Springfield, Massachusetts.

In August of 1954, I arrived for football practice at the college. The small neat brick buildings, the long gentle walkways, the library, and the students from towns and backgrounds I couldn't even imagine, all seemed exotic. This new world was beautiful and frightening.

I was 17.

My father drove me right up to the practice field. He strode up to the coach, Henry Butova, threw my bags at his feet and said, "This kid plays football. He has a full scholarship. If he doesn't work out, send him home." Then he turned and walked away.

I was on my own. I had never been out in the world before. So I used the only tools I'd brought with me: ambition and determination.

I practiced relentlessly. The coach was encouraging and sympathetic. I made first-string quarterback.

My life plan seemed to be working until my third year when I broke my wrist while playing hockey against Princeton. In those days you didn't get carried along on your scholarship until you were well enough to play again. I was out of school. I went back to Hudson. I took night courses, and exercised my splintered wrist. I had to find a way to play. Then, in the winter of 1957, my doctor told me I'd never throw a football again.

I proved the doctor wrong. Returning for my senior year at the bottom of the heap, forced to go through summer try-outs and practice, I made both the football and the hockey teams. I became an All-American. In October of that year I was being scouted by the pros; the Patriots picked me on the tenth round of the draft. Me, a small guy with a stiff wrist.

No one has ever been as euphoric as I was, or as ripe for a fall.

I committed the first of two major screwups in my life. I got lazy, smug, over-confident. I thought I'd made it to the top of the mountain, so I took it easy. I didn't practice as hard as I once had. I lasted two weeks in the Patriots' preseason camp.

At that moment, my entire life's dream disappeared. I had failed. My father, with his stern love, seemed unapproachable. I didn't know how I could face those who had so many dreams invested in me.

After all, I was just a kid, like my kids or yours.

Never before had I been forced to admit such failure. But I learned a valuable lesson from that moment of defeat. It made me realize that there was strength in acknowledging a failure with no excuses. So, I didn't cop a plea. I didn't say, "I'm too small, my wrist is too badly injured." I went home and said, "I messed up. I wasn't good enough. Now I have to go on from here."

When I think back I remember a lot of confusion and fear. I was so afraid of failing.

Today, it helps me understand the pressure that our kids live under, the pressures that prevent them from being able to reach out and say, "Hey, I made a mistake. Help me."

But it took me years to come to that understanding.

What I've come to see—age has to have its rewards—is that Hudson, Massachusetts and my family gave me a great foundation. Hudson was small and tough like my dad, but it was also caring and protective like my mother.

Everyone in town knew each other. If your dad wasn't around to discipline you, some other father would step in to do the job. If you needed a meal or some attention, all the mothers were there to provide care. Teachers cared and helped; they became your best friends. The whole town knew what you did and cared about what happened to you.

My father is gone now, but he grumbled and fought to the end. He never gave an inch to the world until he had to. Thank you, Dad. You taught me that we can accomplish miracles once we see they are the stuff of ordinary life: love, work and determination.

Now, the SADD program has taken the lessons that Hudson taught its children and proved them to be as reliable as ever. Hard work and responsibility for those around you are the seeds that were planted in me by my early days.

They are the same seeds that flowered into the grass-roots movement that is SADD.

A New Life

My failure at the Patriots taught me a lot, but it took me a while to absorb the lessons. After I was cut I headed off on a slightly sloppy course. I played slapshot hockey in Canada. I lived slipshod on a personal level. But finally I settled into coaching, teaching and counseling. And I met Carol.

Delicate, blonde, high-spirited and brave, Carol entered my life like a glowing package of light and beauty. Her strength of character awed me. She was supportive without being self-effacing. She was a person to be reckoned with. And she was willing to accept a ragged-edged, hot-tempered young man.

We are all blessed if we can have true beauty enter our lives once. I was and have been continually blessed by Carol. From the first days of our marriage she has provided the wise guidance and unwavering support I needed. I am the character up front. She is the rock, the hope, my inspiration. She is my best friend.

Carol, who was also a teacher, and I moved into our first and only house in Marlboro, Massachusetts. I took a teaching job at nearby Framingham. The school system was progressive and supportive. I set up the first alcohol and drug counseling programs in the state.

I felt terrific.

What I didn't know was that my motives were selfish, that I was simply trying to fulfill my own ambitions. My activities seemed directed towards helping kids. Oh, I was trying, but I didn't help my students as much as I thought I did.

The sixties were a rough time for all of us. Families were bewildered by the quickly changing social mores. Kids were floundering without enough direction or discipline. It was a time when the family and society no longer provided an ironclad set of rules for kids to live by or rebel against. In place of the rules we'd grown up with was a "do your own thing" attitude. So many kids in the school system seemed to have nothing to rely on.

I tried to give them somewhere to go. The Framingham High School counseling center and our home were open to them all, at all hours of the day and night. Carol and I found ourselves with an extended family of troubled kids. We started our own wonderful family at the same time; Willy was our first-born.

How do you describe your first son? Me, Mr. Tough, was mush inside. I loved having a child. I loved having a world at home that was open to the troubled kids in school, yet free from their troubles. Carol and I worked to avoid in our family the mistakes we saw around us.

Carol never complained, even when we turned the basement into an emergency crash pad for burnt-out kids. Some nights the phone would ring at two A.M. and I'd have to run out and save some kid in an acid-crazed frenzy from jumping off a bridge. I confess I didn't know how frightening it was for her until years later when she told me, "Sometimes I didn't know who was sleeping in the house or what they might do. I was afraid they'd hurt Willy. It was so frightening to see those kids in such pain. I'd look at Willy and cry that the world might offer him such pain, too."

But I didn't really know this. I was doing what I believed would make the world a better place. I was being the ever-reliable Mr. A. I was buying my own line of counseling and never questioning its effectiveness.

Carol argues that I'm too hard on myself about those years, that the proof of the program is in the results. She points out to me that so many of the kids we knew then are family friends today. They have grown and thrived and have their own children. We are like grandparents to them.

But late at night I still cry for those who slipped away.

In the 1970–71 school year, I was selected as the Massachusetts Teacher of the Year. I was flying high. It was a moment of pride that erased whatever residue of disappointment I carried about failing in professional sports.

I filled my classrooms with young people who were eager for help. They listened to me deliver the facts about drugs and alcohol, but then they went right back out and did drugs and alcohol.

My lectures didn't work, but I didn't see it.

The kids might just as well have said, "Thanks a lot, teacher, but I learned all that in the fifth grade. I am very bright. I can understand all about drugs. I know more about them than you do. But I've got to get going, so excuse me now. I'm going to do my thing. I'm going to drink and drive. Bye."

The kids I counseled after school paid no more mind to my lectures than my students did. But I kept delivering the lectures. Even when one kid on acid had to be talked down from a suicide perch, and another had to be given mouth to mouth resuscitation after taking an overdose of pills, I kept believing that my words would change their lives. Oh, I saved some lives with emergency rescues, but that's no act of greatness. It's a last resort.

But I didn't see it. Not then.

Right after the Teacher of the Year Award I accepted a job with the Wayland Public Schools as an administrator and hockey coach. Kids were my joy. Being a coach brings you closer to the boys on your team than you can imagine. They are their happiest, saddest, most intensely personal during practice, on the field and in the locker room. You are with them at every test of their character and strength. They trust you and depend on you, and you care about all aspects of the players' lives because you can't be effective in sports if you are self-destructive in other parts of your life.

These kids were counseled on drugs and alcohol as a part of the daily athletic routine. I believed they were with me. Every love has its blind spots, but I believed I was exempt from that problem. I had dedicated my life to seeing, and to telling. I believed I really saw what was going on in the world.

During these years my own family grew into a complex and wonderful tangle. Jeffrey was born a year and a half after Willy. By 1971 Mark was on the scene. What was obvious to Carol and me was that each child was unique. Willy was always easy-going but quietly determined to stand up for himself; Jeffrey, wise beyond his years, saw into the dynamics of personalities like a sage; and Mark, "small boy," Carol calls him, was just as good and sweet as possible.

My kids provided me with daily lessons in, well, frankly, humility. I mean, just when I'd work myself up into one of those fatherly rages that are supposed to make everyone toe the line and live a life of virtue (you know the speech), they'd shoot me down.

I'll never forget the day Carol and I were having a disagreement. I threw my hands up in the air, rolled my eyes and looked over at Willy as if to say, "Can you believe this?" And do you know what he said?

"Don't look at me, Dad. She's your wife. She's just my mother."

It killed me.

He was right. My relationship with Carol was distinct from his relationship with her. He saw her differently, and was not able or willing to agree or disagree with me about what I thought was going on.

At that moment I saw just how complicated a family's set of relationships are. Each child deserves to be treated as an individual. When I hear parents say, "Why is my son so touchy when I treat him exactly like his brother?" I know that the answer is in the question.

You can't treat each kid in a family the same way; each child must be loved and respected for his or her uniqueness.

The web of relationships in a family is a complicated and delicate thing.

Willy has a separate relationship with Carol and with me. We are not a single entity; we are each individuals to him. Furthermore, he has his own special relationship to his two, very different, younger brothers.

Jeffrey, the middle child, not only has his special relationships with me and with Carol, he also relates to one younger and one older brother. No one else in the family has the relationships he does.

Mark, the youngest, has his set of unique relationships with each of his two older brothers and with his parents.

Then Carol has her relationships. I have mine.

Each of us has four family relationships that are unique. There are, all together, twenty relationships being conducted under one roof in the small and ordinary Anastas family! Your family has its own comparable network.

It's a wonder we can all fit at the dinner table.

Our family grew, as yours has. I reveled in my work. I was proud of my family. I really felt I had learned my lessons from life. I eased up on the fear and ambition that I'd used as a defense to survive my teen years. I'd grown with Carol. I believed I'd learned a lesson or two about handling the tough realities of life, but with the deaths of John and Buddy I confronted tragedy that I had never imagined. It made me question the quality of my teaching abilities, and even the quality of my character and my convictions.

I had spent the past twenty-two years working with kids. I had been rewarded for my progressive approach to alcohol and drug counseling. I had filled my ambitions and ego with the pleasure of being recognized as a leader in the field. I was supposed to be doing it right.

But at that time I had to admit I had personally failed the two boys.

This was one foul-up I could not escape.

All the toughness and sense of responsibility my father had given me, all the insight I had struggled to gain since I was cut from the Patriots, all the compassion I believed I lived by, all the wisdom I thought I taught my students, had failed to stop these incredible tragedies.

Founding SADD is the one gift that I can look to for

consolation. None of us have to go through what Buddy and John's friends and parents went through. No child has to die as Buddy and John died. Because, now, each of us has the power to take those boys' sacrifices and turn them into the gift of life.

I am fortunate to have been in a position to establish a movement such as SADD. My life story may explain why I have dedicated myself to John and Buddy's memory and to SADD, but your life is fuel for your energetic dedication to helping your family and community, too.

Through SADD, we can all reach out our hands and join together to say with quiet resolve: *Never again! Never again!*

** 5 **

Special Friends

I have been surrounded by heroes. That is what has allowed me to do things far beyond my natural capacity. My family, my friends, the kids of this country, the early supporters of SADD have all given me their strength. It has allowed me to leave behind the security of my teaching position and find a way to make my dream a reality for all the kids in America.

The response to that first rally in Wayland was what convinced me that our fledgling organization was going to elicit a large national response. Teachers from all over the country contacted Wayland for information. Kids wrote to me asking for my help. Parents called and begged me to come speak to their children.

I had to respond to the cry for help that SADD unleashed.

I could not continue teaching and make that response. So I arranged for a two-year leave of absence from the school system, and with no secure funding, I began SADD.

This meant I was risking my own security, and my children's future. The kids and Carol were not demanding, but they had a right to expect that their lives would not be too badly disrupted. If I was to make this move it had to be a family commitment. They had the right and power to veto the decision. We held a meeting.

The dining room in our house in Marlboro is graced with Carol's handiwork. She painted the colonial stencils on the walls, and created the fine arrangements of decorations and pictures. The table, which held us together through so many meals and family discussions, is big and shiny. With everyone seated around it, however, there is not much floor space. I found it difficult to pace, but pace I did, in a circle, back and forth, around and around. I told the family:

"I believe that SADD is going to work. I believe that kids all over the country have woken up and are clamoring for such an organization. In my heart, I have to follow their call. I owe it to John and Buddy. I owe it to you kids. But I could be wrong. It could be a dream. I don't know.

"If I work at SADD full-time it will mean that we won't have the income we have right now. I can't promise that you will be able to live like we have been living, but I swear I won't let you down. I will find a way.

"Money can't buy happiness. But this dream I have can create a happier world for all of us.

"What should I do?"

My family's response was overwhelming. Mark simply asked if he could still have the bicycle he wanted. Jeffrey and Willy saw that I was serious and agreed. Carol added a resounding "Do it!"

The family was unified (even if it was a little terrified by the wild-eyed father it saw before them). For that I am grateful.

It was settled. All that remained was to secure funding for SADD so I could follow the call of the kids across the country.

Early Friends

Since the meeting in Orlando when I had brought the SADD idea to my colleagues, William Plymat had been working to introduce me to many people who might support SADD. In addition I had been in contact with my friend Otto Moulton, a leader in the National Federation of Parents for Drug-Free Youth. He was the first person to offer help, in the form of a $2,000 personal loan, to keep SADD going during the summer of 1982. I will never forget his generosity. He is a gentle and trusting friend.

Plymat, however, had bigger dreams. He was concerned with creating an ongoing financial basis for the entire organization.

By late spring, when Wayland had the first SADD week, Massachusetts had offered us a grant through Paul McHugh of the State Highway Safety Commission. It allowed us to print 500 copies of the SADD curriculum for distribution to school systems across the state.

Meanwhile, President Reagan had formally introduced his President's Commission on Drunk Driving in April of 1982. This important body of distinguished men and women, chaired by former Massachusetts Governor John Volpe, was to formulate national policy recommendations on drinking and driving. William Plymat was one of the members.

We did not miss the chance to bring SADD to the attention of this powerful group.

Plymat brought me to Governor Volpe's home. We sat for an hour and a half in his study and hit it off immediately. From that first meeting Volpe and SADD have been connected. Not only did Plymat and former Governor Volpe arrange for me to speak about my program in front of the whole commission, John endorsed the program publicly and in fact went on to become our honorary, but very active, board chairman.

As summer 1982 approached and Carol and the kids prepared to go up to Maine to our beach house, I hunkered down into a weekday bachelorhood that was punctuated by a thousand phone calls, many meetings and far too many TV dinners.

During this chaotic time I was meeting with small groups of kids and parents. It also became clear that, as funding began to come in, SADD needed to be incorporated as a nonprofit organization. This meant that I needed to form a board of directors.

I wanted a group of people that were not just figureheads. I knew that people were not going to believe in SADD and accept it as a national organization just because Bob Anastas said it was good. I needed people on the board who would be recognized for their expertise and were well-respected by their communities—the cream of the crop.

To that end, I solicited support from a cross section of prominent people: a university-based educator, a representative of the conservative branch of the alcohol-abuse organizations, a representative of the liquor trade industry, a politician, a secondary school educator, a representative of corporate America and a concerned parent. No one I approached turned down the position.

The first board of SADD was composed of: Honorary Chairman, John Volpe, former governor of Massachusetts and chairman of President Reagan's Commission on Drunk Driving; William Plymat, founder of Preferred Risk Insurance and cofounder of ACAP; Dr. Alan Cohen, executive director of the Pacific Institute, a research-consulting firm; Don Shea, the vice president of the United States Brewers Association; Dr. Gail Milgram of Rutgers, a leader in college-level training of alcohol and drug counselors; Otto Moulton, industrialist and member of the National Federation of Parents for Drug-Free Youth; and Phillip Anastas, my brother and respected elementary school principal for twenty-five years.

These men and women were essential throughout the beginning of the program; because of them the fledgling project had a chance to really take off. Because we are all so involved in the area of alcohol and drug abuse we found our paths crossed in other organizations as well.

Plymat, now a member of my board, the President's Commission, ACAP, and other related groups, continued to work to find funding for SADD. The exposure he and Volpe afforded me at the commission led to contacts in other government agencies, such as Richard Schweiker of Health and Human Services and the National Transportation Safety Board director, Ray Peck.

In SADD's quest for funding I was to learn lessons I hadn't imagined and suffer the pains of anyone who clings to hopes that are unrealistic.

HHS offered encouragement. But NTSB, through Ray Peck, spoke of direct funding. We expected a $45,000 grant. We were even told over the months that the check was in the mail; but it never came.

We have ultimately realized that federal assistance in the form of grants (which are usually for research) or contracts (which are bid on to fund specific projects) would not fit SADD's organization. But at the time the amount of hope we invested in that promised sum made the program's existence seem very perilous as we waited for what we thought was our life's blood.

While we were learning about the political ins and outs of Washington, we were also finding that the alcohol and drug abuse field itself was torn by political factions. There are those groups that believe that even rehabilitation programs are bad since they offer kids a solution other than abstinence to drug problems. There are those who think that kids should not be allowed to run their own organizations. There are those who condemn dealing with the liquor trade industry at any time, and there are those who want to promote their leader as a personality instead of their cause as a crusade.

While adults sit in their upholstered chairs wrangling about some technicality, our children are dying. It makes no sense to object to saving a life! If kids were not bombarded daily by the temptations and stresses of our society, it might work to say "No, don't" and be done with it. The reality of our world is that 87 percent of all kids in high school have had a drink by the time they graduate. We can look at the long view and strive to change that reality, but we must also deal with the consequences of that reality *today*.

I believe that the preservation of a life must always come

before the preservation of an abstract idea. If you haven't got life you have no use for the idea!

Luckily, Plymat (and I) did not waste too much time arguing with our colleagues or waiting for the federal funding.

The events that took place between late spring and November of 1982 were fast and furious. I was suddenly jumping from one strange airport to another, meeting with large groups of strangers, talking to thousands of new friends. Today, when Carol and I review the chronology of those early days we often disagree about the timing. "You were in Arizona," she'll insist. "I know it was Washington, D.C.," I'll counter. Our only accurate resource is the cluttered pages of the calendars that we have tucked away in the nooks and crannies of our house.

When the summer holiday was over Carol was thrown back into the already frantic world of running the house and taking care of the boys' busy school and social schedules. This year, however, she had double duty.

Carol, who was unprepared to run an office or manage a business, was forced to improvise and juggle with the meager supplies and funds that SADD had. She literally used an old blue shoebox to store her index cards. She took phone calls at all times of the day and night, arranged my travel, acted as a public relations expert, and kept the three boys healthy, happy and well-fed. I was totally spent from the grueling demands of a life lived out of a suitcase and she was exhausted by the demands of a life run out of a shoebox!

"Mom would feel bad when she was too tired to fix us a big breakfast in the morning," Willy recalls. "I would get up, get breakfast and then wake her so she could drive us to school. She would have been working half the night on SADD. I think it was very hard on her."

Many nights, as late as midnight, Carol would be surprised by phone calls from distraught parents and concerned students. They would ask if they could speak with me; but I'd be off in some far-flung corner of the country, working with the new SADD groups. When she'd tell them I wasn't available, they'd begin to pour their hearts out to her.

Her compassion and concern were enormous; she made friends during those first months with many people whom she has still never met in person.

Late at night, with the boys sleeping and the day's housework and SADD business piling up around her, Carol often felt overwhelmed. I was rarely home, and when I'd return, road-weary but exhilarated, we'd barely get to say hello before I'd be off again to tell the tale of John and Buddy and SADD once again.

"I had been used to having Bob around all the time," Carol says. "I mean not only did I suddenly have a full-time job running the SADD office, but I had to take care of the kids and the house, and worry about Bob on top of it. Sometimes late at night, I'd wonder: What about me? But then I'd remember John and Buddy and the incredible response Bob was getting from the kids across the country, and I'd dive right back into the latest stack of mail."

THREE

The Voices of Our Children

From one end of this country to the other teenagers began to speak up: They told the politicians in Washington just what they should do about drinking and driving; they told their parents and their teachers just how important it is to face the problems and pressures that confront the youth of America; they told one another that they loved and cared for their brothers and sisters; and they told me that SADD was going to be one organization that they would stick with, if I would stick with them.

—**Robert Anastas**

6

On the Road

I met so many wonderful students and supporters the first year I traveled across the country that it made all the long days and lonely nights worth it. From the first contacts I had with the members of the President's Commission to the kids whom I spoke with everywhere, every person who heard the SADD message and joined in the crusade became a source of inspiration and friendship.

While Carol held the organization together I was getting so that I didn't know the name of the next town I'd be in. I was lucky to remember my own name! Day after day, airport after airport, I'd go from one meeting to the next. Not only was I answering the kids' call, I was still dealing with government and private industry to work out the basic organization of SADD.

My calendar for the months of September, October and November 1982 shows how frantic my schedule was!

September 8: Boston, Massachusetts. State House. Appearance before a partial assembly of the President's Commission on Drunk Driving.

September 13, 14: Phoenix, Arizona. Presidential Commission Meeting.

September 17: Happy Hollow, North Carolina. Address to the American Council on Alcohol Problems.

September 27: Washington, D.C. Five Massachusetts SADD students and I go with Otto Moulton to meet Secretary of Health and Human Services, Richard Schweiker. Establishment of a Youth Conference on Drinking and Driving.

October 10–12: Washington, D.C. Address the annual meeting of The National Federation of Parents for a Drug-Free Youth.

October 14: Canton, Massachusetts. Canton High School assembly.

October 15: Lakeville, Massachusetts. Lakeville High School assembly.

October 18: Stoughton, Massachusetts. Stoughton High School assembly.

October 19: Litchfield, Connecticut. Litchfield High School assembly.

October 20: Attelboro, Massachusetts. Attelboro High School assembly.

October 21: Neptune, New Jersey. Msgr. Donovan High School assembly.

October 23: Boston, Massachusetts. Women's Christian Temperance Union.

October 24–26: Boca Raton, Florida. The annual president's meeting of the United States Brewers Association.

October 27–30: Naples, Florida. Meeting with Naples Informed Parents and local schools throughout the area.

October 31–November 6: Statewide sweep of Iowa.

November 10: Harrisburg, Pennsylvania. Central Pennsylvania SADD Conference in conjunction with the state. Fourteen school districts participated.

November 15: Long Island, New York. Longwood High School assembly.

That is just a slice of the incredible traveling I have done in the last years. Because it was the first push, the first time I took my idea out to be tested, each and every contact I made has a special place in my memories.

Bill Plymat, to whom I had been talking throughout the spring, was to continue to be the key to meeting a wide range of important political and business connections.

In Arizona he introduced me to Ken Levine, the vice president of Seagrams, Terry Baxter of GEICO insurance and Jim Kemper of Kemper Insurance. It was quite a scene—this fired-up guy from Hudson, Massachusetts socializing with some of the most elegant representatives of corporate America. But we all got along very well and the result was the beginning of solid funding commitments from them to SADD.

Over and over Bill Plymat helped SADD. He was able at every turn to find the way to bridge the disagreements between different groups and take a common stand for the young people of this country. When the first seating of the President's Commission on Drunk Driving in Washington took place, Plymat had arranged for me to attend as his "assistant" and present the SADD case to the assembly.

Let me paint the picture.

The commission, made up of some of the most distinguished men and women in America, was seated in a great paneled room; there were almost as many microphones as people. Reporters clustered outside. The list of distinguished speakers was long and impressive. I was determined to get the SADD message across in the short time I had, and a little awed to find myself in such company.

The Honorable John Volpe, whom I had met earlier that year at his house in suburban Boston, called me forward. I had written a prepared statement and submitted it to the committee, but I'm not really good at toeing the line, even when it's my own line. I began speaking from the text, but as my emotions built up I looked up at each of the commission members and said, just as I would to the kids, "I believe we

69

can stop this number-one killer of young people, drinking and driving. I know the kids can do it. They have the power. We have to let them do this. I don't have proof that it will work; we have just started. But I have seen the faces of the students and heard their passionate responses to SADD. I promise you that if I am given a chance to get this off the ground I will come back to you in three years and you'll have the proof. SADD will save lives."

They didn't doubt me.

I was right.

Bill Plymat had lined up all kinds of organizations and people as potential supporters of SADD. Each one, from the United States Brewers Association, to DISCUS, to the Wine Institute, was testimony to his broadminded commitment to forming a coalition that would work together, laying aside smaller philosophical differences, to help the kids of this country.

One of the most dramatic and effective examples of Bill's sense of detente was his approach to the United States Brewers Association (USBA). Although Bill is a long-time leader of the conservative, pro-abstinence wing of the alcohol use and abuse organizations, he sent these representatives of the liquor trade industry information on SADD, with the request that they consider funding support.

Don Shea, now president of the organization, but then vice president in charge of educational programs, and Henry King, then president, were impressed and surprised.

"It's a testimony to his being able to transcend his personal philosophy and help the kids of this country. He is a very special man," states Mr. Shea.

Don Shea immediately grasped the SADD message and asked Bill to arrange for me to meet him when I was at the commission hearing. From that first brief meeting, we set up an appointment for Don to fly to Boston in July for in-depth discussions. Don was really coming to check out SADD and see if it was a viable organization. An hour and a half in

Wayland was all it took to convince him that he was in the presence of an important idea and a solid project.

Well, Shea may have been checking on SADD, but I was equally curious about the USBA. I wanted to be sure that the USBA was good enough for SADD.

I asked Don the following three questions:

"Do you believe that illegal drinking by kids should stop?"

"Do you want to vanquish the number-one killer of our young people?"

"Am I to believe that you are parents, not just business people?"

The USBA and Don answered, "Yes. Yes. Yes."

That's when I knew we could work together. And since that time I have never met a person in the liquor trade industry who wants kids drinking illegally, or driving drunk and dying.

(One funny personal note: When Don got home to Washington he told his wife, Vicky, that he'd met with me. It turned out that I had been her history teacher in Framingham North High School!)

From those exhilarating first contacts the funding base for SADD began to take shape.

There were others on this early road who found SADD a worthy cause. Lawrence Williford of Allstate offered an "in kind" grant to cover all our printing material expenses. Allstate made the best designers and production services available to us so that we could distribute our information to schools and students at no charge. Without them our words would have floated away on the wind, but because of their help we were able to blanket the country with the printed message.

I won't claim we were an organization yet! Carol was still sharing the phone with our three sons, still filing our calendars in a shoebox and still trying to buy enough office supplies with the shoestring budget we had, but I could begin to see that my idea was in fact going to take off.

The next big break came when I was invited to speak before the USBA President's annual meeting in Boca Raton that October.

This speech was crucial because I wanted to impress these people with the fact that they were a good candidate for a partnership with SADD.

After my speech Carol and I were seated at the table of August Busch of Anheuser Busch. This first contact was arranged by Steve Lambright. Mr. Busch was extremely caring and sympathetic to my cause. I pressed SADD's case to Mr. Busch. He asked me several pointed questions about the organization; he even asked me what my budget would be for the projected year. When I told him, I saw a puzzled look on his face. He was probably thinking, "How can this man expect to run a national program on such a small budget?" I really think Mr. Busch liked my determination and spirit; I know I liked his willingness to confront tough issues and his sense of social responsibility. He has been a solid supporter of SADD ever since. I respect and admire this man. I would like to make it very clear to all those people who feel that if programs such as mine take money from the liquor trade industry, it seems to be money from "People you can't trust." Anheuser Busch has never exercised any biased influence, neither have people from the Wine Institute, the House of Seagrams or Stroh's Beer, among others. In fact, if it were not for the early support of people in the liquor trade industry SADD would not have succeeded on such a broad scale. There are thousands of kids alive because these people cared enough to not only voice their support but also give their financial help.

When our kids said "Help us help ourselves," unselfish people could not turn away.

New Groups and Early Friends

Right after the Boca Raton meeting I was scheduled to go to Naples, Florida to meet with the Naples Informed Parents organization and our wonderful friend, Mary Peterson. She had heard about SADD and called Carol. To this day they have never met, but over the phone they forged a friendship that has endured.

Her group was part of a growing network of concerned parents organizations. Mary knew that the one key element they lacked was the participation of the students.

"Otto Moulton, who knew Bob, had made us aware of SADD very early on," Mary recalls. "So when I got ahold of Carol, I asked if Bob could visit five schools in our area. I put a muzzle and a leash on him and dragged him everywhere, through the swamps of the Everglades to a tiny little high school and into larger metropolitan areas."

I don't remember needing a muzzle and a leash, but I do remember being really wired up. I'd brought along a student from Canton, Massachusetts, and we worked. Boy, did we work.

From that effort we now have SADD in six area high schools in Florida plus some junior high participation. Mary has continued to really keep the kids active and interested. Their Dri-Hi Project Graduation efforts are particularly wonderful.

I didn't have two seconds to recover from the exhausting Boca Raton–Naples trip. When I got home Carol washed my socks, fed me a meal and pointed me towards Iowa where Plymat and many concerned educators had put together a week-long swing through the state.

I landed in Des Moines on the evening of October 31. I guess my Halloween costume was to look like the most tired but most exhilarated man on earth.

Plymat met me at the airport and laid out the schedule for me. Working with the Iowa State High School Athletic Association and with a wonderful man named Bernie Saggau, I was to speak to a conference of more than 400 high school students representing thirty-five schools.

"SADD has made a dramatic difference in our state," says Saggau. "The year before the SADD conference we had forty-six deaths on our roads because of drunk driving. A year after it was down to twenty-nine."

Dewitt Jones, the principal of Norwalk High School, heard me and made what Bernie Saggau calls "a ramrod commitment to SADD." Mr. Jones comments: "Our youngsters got a hold of it and carried the ball. SADD is a great idea and without it the death rate would have climbed in the state."

Mr. Jones has every reason to feel he made a real contribution. When Reagan's Commission wanted to hear from student representatives of SADD it chose the group from Norwalk High School to represent the entire state.

I finished up in Iowa with a sense of incredible joy. These kids, who had come from small schools all over, were definitely committed to setting up SADD chapters across the state.

"When Bob got home," Carol recalls, "he was so energized. He hadn't had a break in months and had to turn around and go to Pennsylvania and Indiana. But he was happy."

The joy was short-lived; a few short days later I was called to bear witness to an awful tragedy when Pat and Tom Valle called from Long Island. Nine students had died in a single car crash over the Labor Day weekend. The Valles were frightened and determined to prevent such a thing from recurring. They took the time and initiative to get the first Long Island parent and student groups going. From our very emotional first contact, it became clear that Long Island was literally dying for SADD. The amount of drunk driving accidents that the various high schools had experienced was frighteningly large. Nassau and Suffolk counties were lucky, however, to have responsive county governments. With the cooperation of Steve Liss of Nassau's Department of Drug and Alcohol Addiction Education Unit and Burke Sampson of the Suffolk agency, SADD was able to create a network of support organizations. The high schools were forming new chapters right and left.

In Nassau, a large conference was set up through Liss and SADD. Held at Longwood High School, it attracted State Senator "Cadillac" Smith from Albany and officials from local communities. Representatives from many high schools attended as well as interested parents and teachers. The feeling in the massive auditorium was electric.

Great kleigs poured white light from the thirty-foot ceiling down onto the packed bleachers that lined two walls of the gymnasium in Longwood High School. Two thousand kids sat shoulder to shoulder on the wooden benches and settled in cross-legged along the shiny basketball floor to hear me speak about a subject they had been lectured on before. I had faced smaller assemblies, I would come to face far larger ones, but my first year I had not yet seen such a crowd.

"Can I do it?" the voice of fear in my head demanded.

"These are your kids . . . kids who you know have the will to live," said another more confident voice.

"But can you get their attention?" poked the voice of fear one more time.

"Hey, they have the power, the energy, the answers. They are waiting to be asked. They will respond," replied my confident half.

I never work on a stage if I can help it; I don't like to be above the kids. I just walk out to a microphone on the floor, look them in the eye, and begin.

The meeting at Longwood took place in the earliest days of SADD when I had been giving my speech to the kids for only a short while. I had not yet found the words I wanted to express my thoughts and feelings. Every time I stood up in front of a group I was experimenting, groping, learning from the spirit of the kids.

I had planned to give my regular twenty-minute speech on alcohol and alcoholism. I sat and waited to be introduced. The other dignitaries delivered their talks. The kids were respectful but seemed to be losing interest.

A sixteen-year-old boy walked to the front of the assembly. He turned and looked back at all the speakers and said: "With all due respect to you, you could raise the drinking age to 55 to match the speed limit and it wouldn't do a thing to keep kids from drinking, and drinking and driving. Until *we* believe that *we* have the power and motivation it's not going to work."

The young man turned his attention back to the audience and went on with his formal introduction.

"Now I'd like to introduce Bob Anastas. He is here to talk to us about death and dying."

75

I stood up. This kid had just demolished my speech! No way was I going to plod through my prepared text. He had said that kids needed power, needed motivation! He had said I would talk on death and dying. . . .

I looked out at the fresh young faces of the audience. I began talking. I spoke about all the trauma that kids go through with their peers and their parents. I asked the kids questions and they shouted answers. I brought them up to the front with me. We gave the talk together!

I felt like I was riding a bronco, and when I was done the response was thunderous. All the kids stood up on their feet, joined hands, and pledged that they would tear down the walls of the Death Box.

That is how the talk I give today was forged. I still get just as excited when I speak to a new group of kids as I did that day at Longwood. The issues and ideas are still fresh; the kids still work with me; I still learn new things from them every time. But I never forget the feelings I had that first day. No matter how accustomed I get to meeting groups and dealing with the media I always carry some of the electricity and shared commitment that Longwood gave me into every new situation.

7

Spotlights and Glare

SADD is a powerful organization of students. I am their spokesperson. I am not a celebrity, I am a worker. But the whirlwind that built up around the success of SADD brought me and my family into the national spotlight in a way we neither expected nor were ready to deal with. Some of the attention was pleasing. It felt like rewards for grueling amounts of work. It also helped SADD claim its rightful place as a focal point of the national concern about drinking, and drinking and driving. But much of it took a toll in little ways on each of us individually.

By the time we had set up SADD chapters in well over half the states and had moved onto a more secure financial footing, I was getting a lot of media attention. There was no way around it. I was the spokesperson, the only spokesperson (until Paul Pacifico joined us in the spring of 1983) who was available to spread the word to the schools. My picture appeared alongside local newspaper articles. I was featured in the first public service announcements. I was the man to talk to about funding and policy. The spotlight and glare were hard to adjust to.

I see what the cult of celebrity does to our young people. They grow up with the illusion, constantly reinforced in the media, that life can be as carefree and empty as a commercial. They aspire to the accomplishments of people who are rewarded handsomely for how they appear or how cool they can be.

Despite my ability to stand up in front of a crowd of two thousand strangers and pour my heart out, I am an intensely private person. I think of myself as very ordinary. Yet few of us, myself included, are totally free of the temptation to join the glossy bandwagon.

My sons reveled in my newfound celebrity. "I figured when these heavy people were calling him that he must be pretty important," Jeffrey admitted. I felt the thrill that comes with the rewards that our society gives to those who have accomplished something.

I am careful to always be on guard; nothing should benefit anyone but the kids who make SADD work; no company should benefit from their support of SADD. I will not put myself before the SADD kids, and I will not be courted, used or exploited by any group or organization.

The first appearance of the public service announcements (PSAs) on national television was a thrill to us all. Those PSAs, which brought the SADD message to a mass audience, were a real turning point in the growth of the organization. None of us expected the kind of air play and attention they garnered; all across the country stations ran them during prime time, many times a day. Added to the locally produced PSAs that the individual SADD chapters were doing for their local radio and TV stations, the slogan "Friends Don't Let Friends Drive Drunk" and other SADD messages were becoming part of the American vocabulary.

Our next national PSA, in the summer of 1983, featured Dallas Cowboy star Drew Pearson. When he turned to the camera and said to kids and their parents, "I've signed a lot of contracts in my life but this is a Contract for Life!" you could feel the electricity he generated.

Soon after that the United States Brewers Association funded three more spots that featured the SADD message. Those spots are still running today!

Finally, in 1984, Patrick Productions made three more PSAs: one featuring a party situation, one highlighting the Contract for Life and one set in a cemetery.

In January and February of 1984 both the Dear Abby and Ann Landers columns printed the Contract for Life, and suggested to all their readers that they request a copy for their families from SADD. The results were astounding! We received eight thousand letters asking for contracts the first week, and postal service trucks were pulling up to the SADD office with more than a thousand letters a day for the next six weeks. We were overjoyed and overwhelmed. Luckily, the local Marlboro Junior Woman's Club sent over many volunteers to help us handle the load. Those compassionate and wonderful women contributed enormously to SADD's growth and helped save lives all over the country.

Meanwhile Carol and the kids were having to deal with the fact that their name and my face appeared regularly on TV and in print. They lost some of their privacy, but all of us were becoming more comfortable with a semi-public role.

"I was always proud," Mark reports. "At school, kids would tell me they'd seen my dad. It was never a problem. They didn't make fun of SADD or me."

By August of 1985 Willy even found it possible to take a public stand and participate in filming a brand-new series of PSAs that were produced by Chuck Neff Productions, the creative force behind our SADD movies such as "You Drink, You Drive, You Die."

I was totally overcome with joy that Willy had the character to stand up in front of the world, and his friends, and say, "Hi, I'm Willy Anastas. You may know my dad, Bob Anastas. I don't drink. I don't need to." My son, who seems in some ways the most reserved member of our family, turned out to be a natural actor. The spots were great.

In 1983, at the same time that the media was heating up, the federal government, a source of both frustration and of support, decided SADD was pretty special. President Reagan issued a proclamation endorsing SADD, and Margaret Heckler, Richard Schweiker's successor at HHS, decided to give me an award for my service to SADD and to the youth of the country.

The National Youth Conference that I had initially worked on in September of 1982 with Schweiker had finally come to fruition. In January of 1983, I traveled from Wayland to Washington with four kids from Wayland, Canton, Massachusetts, and Central Islip, Long Island.

The conference, which was originally going to feature only SADD, had been expanded to include all my friends and other organizations, at my recommendation. Project Graduation, a statewide effort to set up alcohol-free graduation and prom activities, was introduced. So was the Teen Institute, a national summer program that trains kids in communication skills.

This conference marked the ascendancy of SADD as the premier student-run, student self-care organization in the country. I was so proud to hear the kids testify and to see the impact of their ideas.

Margaret Heckler was scheduled to present the award to me before the conference. Unfortunately, I had a previous commitment to a group of kids in Dennison, Iowa, and those kids came first. Carol went to Washington in my place to accept the honor.

The spotlight is not Carol's natural habitat. She has never thought of herself as a person who would be in such a position, but just as quiet Willy turned out to be a natural actor, Carol has the natural grace and force of character to let her waltz through a public ceremony.

There she was, surrounded by some of the nation's most

important politicians. "I am Carol Anastas," she announced from the dais. "I am here to accept this award in place of my husband, Robert Anastas, because he had a very important commitment to the kids at a high school in Dennison, Iowa. It was his first priority. He has asked me to thank all the people who have supported the SADD kids."

The whole family's eventual adjustment to the spotlight and glare came after much rougher exposure to the public eye: the filming of a made-for-TV movie based on our family's life and on John and Buddy's deaths. Written by Peter Silverman for CBS, it was called "The Contract for Life: The SADD Story."

The process of creating a script, of filming and airing the production put all of us through a lot of soul searching.

The fine actors and actresses who made up the cast helped ease our worries about how our family and SADD would be presented. Steven Macht, who portrayed me, was passionately committed to the script. He traveled all over with me, listening to me give my speech, and met the kids. He told me that his role was very important to him because it was a piece of acting that he did not for the money or prestige, but to save lives! That kind of higher sense of purpose helped ease my worries about the right nuances of character and motivation being transmitted.

My kids, however, felt the personal intrusion acutely. Throughout the process they were wary. But now, reflecting on the experience, they have a greater understanding of the positive aspects of the experience. "It gave SADD recognition it needed and that was good," Jeffrey says.

During the actual filming in Hollywood, Carol sat in attendence since I was busy traveling and couldn't find the time. She settled into the studio-poolside scene, and watched to make sure no last-minute changes to the script were necessary.

The afternoon in December 1984 when the movie aired, I left the house. Driving around Marlboro, I was filled with apprehension. How would the SADD kids react? How would John and Buddy's parents feel? How would my own family respond? The restless torment I felt was eating at me but I couldn't face the TV screen and evaluate it for myself. I had to simply let it float out through the airwaves, and find whatever destiny was awaiting it.

The SADD story broke all rating records for its time slot.

It received critical acclaim and an Emmy.

It helped SADD spread its message.

It made my family "famous" for a few minutes.

I was glad for most of the results.

In the midst of all this turmoil our family also had to face a serious crisis. Carol was diagnosed as having breast cancer and had to have a double radical mastectomy. This happened while I was thousands of miles away talking to kids in the West. The boys, with their incredible personal resources of love and compassion, were at Carol's side. I flew home immediately.

The fear and the shock were far-reaching. It is only because of the abilities we have developed over the years to share our thoughts and feelings with one another that we were able to weather the difficult event as well as we did. Carol, who suffered both the physical trauma and the psychological shock that this sort of operation always causes, found that our ability to cry together let us move from the dark fear to hope as quickly as possible. One of the wonderful results was the incredible outpouring of love that she received from SADD kids, workers and friends all over the country.

No family is exempt from life's burdens, but Carol's incredible spirit and her determination to get well have seen her through the worst of times. Today, she is healthy and optimistic about the future. She helped the boys and me regain our hope and optimism, too.

I know of no better example of the benefits of a close and communicating family than the feelings we were all able to share with one another during this frightening episode.

Although I hope that none of you ever has to face such a trauma, you will face it best if you can face it together.

We have become a public family, but we have kept our private lives. We have, each in our own way, helped one another to learn how to accept with dignity all that life presents to us. We don't take the public notice too seriously. We are very committed to keeping the "private" family healthy. The kids, Carol and I are proud we have lived a life that is an example to others. We are happy that we gained some small rewards for our nonstop labors. But mostly, we are delighted that we have never stopped feeling like an ordinary family, one that is simply special because it is our own.

8

The Kids Are All Right

From the beginning the kids have been powerfully committed to SADD. As the organization has spread across the country to more than 8,000 schools I have witnessed the strength and dedication they possess.

No school is more special than any other, no group more deserving of praise. But to illustrate the scope of the kids' activities I am going to share with you three examples of the full force of the grown-up SADD!

Jill Melander, a student at Loveland High School in Loveland, Colorado, is a passionate SADD advocate.

"In the past two years thirteen of my friends have died from car accidents, drinking and suicide! Only two out of the thirteen were because of drinking and driving but it is too horrible. I want to help stop it all," she says with an angry sadness. "I'm tired of going to funerals." Jill explains, "One boy died from exposure and alcohol toxicity after he wandered coatless from a party and got lost in the snow.

"His friends have done their own video about his death and they show it around the state to other schools now. It really gets to you."

There is a bouncy, bright determination in Jill and in her mother, Dee Melander, who is the Colorado State SADD coordinator. Fired by Jill's enthusiasm and the mounting number of tragedies in the community, Dee has been working to promote SADD chapters across the state.

In October 1985, the statewide SADD rally brought over eight hundred parents and student representatives from all over Colorado and Wyoming together at the University of Northern Colorado at Greeley. These kids came by bus from small towns on both sides of the Rockies; they were full of love and enthusiasm. It was one of the most effective, caring, moving conferences I had ever been to, mostly because Dee got involved with SADD. Her motivation is unselfish and sincere, and it translates to the kids; they respond in kind.

In Pueblo, Colorado, Kathy Vukich and her sister are also helping to spread the SADD movement. She reports that throughout her years at South High School it has been apparent that the students really do care about each other.

It is ironic that Jill's was one of the last high schools in the state to get a SADD chapter going.

"Our administration was against SADD at first because they didn't want to recognize that kids were drinking," Jill remembers. "Now that SADD has gone statewide they see that it has great value, and we have our own chapter. I mean, I used to see kids in school with liquor in their lockers! With all the deaths of my friends, my advice to other kids who want to start chapters is to find the people in your school who can stand up for themselves and stick with it."

In North Carolina, kids live in their cars. They drive to school, to play, just for fun. In Greensboro, where Bob Owens is the coach at Northeast Gilford High School, teenagers died almost every year from car accidents.

"We'd feel bad for a while and then somehow we'd forget and it would happen again. In February of 1982 we lost Susan Critz. That accident finally got to me, and I said I've got to do more than pay lip service to the situation. So I gave out my phone number to every kid in school and said, 'Call me any time if you need a ride because you've been drinking or you have to take a ride with someone who has been.' The kids and I decided to contact the National SADD office. They had heard of it and it seemed like it was what we were looking for. We chartered our chapter that month. It was one of the first in the nation.

"Bob sent us the starter kit. We had twenty-five to thirty kids who were members. Today, we have 450!

"When Susan died we had had a death nine years in a row. Since February of 1982 there has not been one. Not one."

Working with local SADD faculty advisors, the North Carolina State SADD coordinator Steve Streeter has been able to get a dramatic improvement in the statistics of deaths due to driving drunk across the entire state.

"I went up to Boston in September of 1983 to meet with Bob and be trained by him," Steve recalls. "Then we were able to work with our governor, James B. Hunt, and launch a statewide effort."

Tim Merrick was president of the Gilford SADD chapter; he is now a college student. During his tenure, and in the following years, Gilford High always had an extensive calendar of events. There is always the designated driver program, and they spend a lot of time all year preparing for Project Graduation. Their efforts are put into a Prom Survival Kit that offers students tips on prom etiquette, restaurant reviews, merchant discount coupons for SADD members, information on the drunk driving laws and on SADD. Because it contains so much useful information everyone always reads it. The Dry-Hi program, with its alternative parties, has also been very popular.

North Carolina is an example of the dramatic impact of active SADD programs. According to Steve Streeter, "The one message I want to get across to kids is 'Reach the beautiful life ahead of you.' "

In North Carolina, SADD—with the help of people like Owens and Streeter and the dedication of students like Tim Merricka, Bobby Smith, Kim Cummings and Chad Hyatt—is helping more and more students to reach that goal.

Many states besides Colorado and North Carolina are now putting together a coordinated campaign to make SADD a part of every school in the state. Michigan, where our state SADD representative, Larry Rotta, also works as a Consultant for Substance Abuse Education to a school district in southeast Michigan, is an example.

Rotta read through our material one afternoon in 1983 and decided that it was just what his kids needed. He arranged for me to come to Michigan to meet over 9,000 students. Each and every one was fired up and ready to act.

This response, which I was seeing week after week, state after state, gave me the most reaffirming, thrilling feeling. The kids were hungering for the opportunity to take charge of their own lives and express their care for one another. In Michigan they had the chance when Larry conducted training programs for students interested in how to start a SADD chapter. Just as many dedicated educators have done, Larry took the initiative to translate the SADD national program into a personalized regional project that reached out and grabbed the kids' attention and helped them focus their energy.

Building on his own enthusiasm and the kids' desire for more support, Larry took a leave of absence in 1984 from the school district to organize SADD chapters across the state. A local businessman supplied funding to finance the year's work and Michigan was ready to take off! Thanks to the combined efforts of the Michigan kids, the state government, local businesses and local and national SADD representatives, there are now over 225 active SADD chapters across the state and the registration rate is holding at three a week!

This team effort has been reinforced by Michigan's great network of support systems across the state. In every county a state Drug and Alcohol Prevention coordinator, Rotta and the central SADD office are in constant communication. Any SADD chapter that needs help, guidance, support or advice can work with their local Prevention coordinator who is well trained in SADD philosophy and techniques. This extensive network of professional advisors puts its biggest effort into keeping the kids themselves at top energy level.

To that end, the local Prevention coordinator in every county holds a monthly meeting of all SADD leaders from each high school. They get together to share problems, discuss future strategies and get the moral support and reaffirmation they need. Once back in their own high schools, the kids can work with their school's SADD faculty advisor to implement their ideas.

Michigan illustrates just how important are faculty advisors. We've found that when the kids choose the advisor, *not the other way around,* it gets the best results. The kids instinctively know which teacher will be the most active, compatible, supportive, and will have time and energy to devote to the kids. The only problem is that those teachers, because they are so good, are also the busiest in the school. To give them a helping hand in Michigan, we have begun working with the statewide Junior Chamber of Commerce (JC). By careful selection and training of a JC member in each town, SADD provides the local faculty advisor with a co-partner if he or she gets overburdened.

Local educators like Todd Johnson of the Kent Intermediate School District are part of the statewide effort to support SADD, for they have spread the word to their kids as well. Todd has watched the effect SADD has on the kids. "When you say to them, 'Hey, no one is going to think badly of you for *not* drinking,' they are suddenly better able to make decisions."

All of these efforts, the active use of a SADD state representative, the network of state-sponsored Prevention coordinators, the use of the JCs and the attention to faculty advisors, keep the SADD chapters strong.

One twelfth grader from Michigan put it best: "There is something different in our school now. Now the whole school is like a community of caring people."

SADD now has thousands of special kids and dynamic chapters. Every one of them deserves praise and mention, but that is not possible here. Instead, I have offered you a small sample of the kind of work that is being done all over, work which has created a whole new set of horizons for SADD. The kids have taken the initiative to spread the SADD message to junior high and university students. SADD now has a junior high school program designed to help kids stay drug-free and alcohol-free. The new SADD university program is designed to help young adults make a healthy transition to an independent, responsible adult life.

** 9 **

New Horizons: Junior High and University SADD Chapters

As SADD becomes a part of every high school experience, we see how important it is for students both younger and older to share the benefits the program provides. Nothing makes me happier than to think SADD can reach out and embrace all our youth, from the preteens to the young adults who are also far too often victims of the tragedy of drinking and driving.

By the fall of 1985 SADD's first "graduating class" had entered its last year in high school. Kids who were freshmen in 1981 when the program first started, who had participated in their local chapters all through high school, were preparing to move out into the college environment. They were our vanguard. The effectiveness of the SADD approach had been proven by them: Deaths in their age group, due to drinking and driving, were down 33%!

This dramatic improvement was coupled with a 10% decline in the overall consumption of alcohol by teenagers as well. We had the statistics I promised Reagan's Commission three years before.

But this was no time to sit back and smile.

The younger brothers and sisters of the SADD graduates had watched and listened to their older siblings. They had seen their parents and their friends' parents opening up to improve communication in their families. They had come to understand that parents had a right to supervise parties, that children had an obligation to supervise themselves.

Maybe, just maybe, these younger brothers and sisters could be spared the nightmare of peer pressure and drinking, and drinking and driving. Perhaps they could all be kept drug-free. Perhaps they could enter their teenage years prepared to act responsibly. The formation of an active SADD Junior High Program was the logical next step.

At the same time, we did not want to dissipate the energy of our graduating SADD members who were moving into the far less structured and supervised world of the university. They would enter the high-pressure world of academia, where a Friday night fraternity beer bash was an institution. The high school seniors asked us for help in carrying on the SADD program to their campuses. They knew that their commitment and concern were important to maintain.

So, in the fall of 1985 SADD began comprehensive work with both college and junior high chapters. Each program offers students and parents a chance to strengthen their commitment to the highest quality of life possible. Let's examine each of them in detail, for they are unique from the high school program in important ways.

Junior High—I'm Special because I'm Me!

The Junior High School program is a chance to establish communication between students, parents and teachers *before* it has broken down. The intimacy that exists between children and parents in elementary school does not have to be lost.

As our children grow, the circles of intimacy that surround them shift from family to friends and acquaintances. Suddenly parents find they are no longer close to their growing children. The loss of communication and understanding with your child is the first step towards exposing your child to the negative effects of peer pressure.

If you've got a child in junior high you'll recognize this scene. Let's take an average kid; we'll call him Mikey. He's thirteen now, but I'm going to take him back to when he was in kindergarten. Mom and Dad were his whole world. When he came home from school Mom hugged him and sat him down to find out everything that happened.

Mikey loved it. "First day, Mom," he says, "and I've got it down pat. I found the right bathroom! I had lunch, I had recess. You know what else, Mommy? I added up one and one and it came to three. But that's okay. Look what the teacher gave me, Mom, a pumpkin on my paper." And what did Mom do? She took the paper and put it right on the refrigerator door! She said, "Michael, you're the genius of the neighborhood!" Mike's papers were all over the refrigerator door; he and his parents were having a lot of fun, and they talked to each other all the time. That communication continued up until about the eighth grade. Then all of a sudden Mike's world got more and more complex. It began to include all kinds of people and experiences that Mom and Dad might not approve of. Mike doesn't think enough of himself (that's part of being an adolescent) to take a chance on getting into a deep discussion about his new world with his parents, and his parents don't ask, they don't even know what there is to ask *about*. Slowly they drift apart, not because Mike does anything wrong, not because they are bad parents, just because they stop using their communication muscles. They get flabby.

This does not have to happen. Unlike high school kids, junior high kids are not yet well on the road to separation from their intimate family circle. They haven't had to bear the full force of high school pressures and traumas alone.

If parents and kids work together, through SADD, from the very beginning of junior high they can build a bridge that will keep the family together, informed and active, so that the kind of repair work that SADD does in high school will not be necessary.

These kids are not yet faced with the peer pressure to experiment with alcohol and drugs that affects their older siblings. They have not yet begun to hide their innermost thoughts and feelings from their families. They have not yet engaged in behavior which they fear will alienate their parents. They are full of excitement and anticipation about their futures.

God knows that junior high is often the roughest time in a child's life. Puberty, with all its associated tension, is a delicate time for both boys and girls, a time when they are truly becoming new people. They are fighting to get a hold of all that it means. They desire independence. They fear independence.

We can help them navigate the pressures of the rest of their lives by offering them the guidance of our wisdom and authority through open communication. We can help them make choices about drugs and alcohol that will free them from those dangers.

The Secret World

The root of all teenage conflict is essentially low self-esteem. The self-abuse that is the root of drug and alcohol consumption comes, in many instances, from a desperate attempt to acquire self-esteem through a kind of negative honor system. "I can be a big guy" and "I'm sophisticated" are attitudes that kids use to deceive themselves about the "virtues" of alcohol and drugs.

Junior high kids don't know that they are wonderful simply because they are whoever they are! They feel so shaky about their status in their peer group that the idea of stepping outside the accepted norms is threatening. That is why the junior high school campaign is conducted under the slogan:

I'M SPECIAL BECAUSE I'M ME.™

We believe that if our preteens can be given the support and confidence they need to see their individual worth then the information we give them about the hazards of alcohol and drugs will be accepted. This will be the beginning of a new graduating class who can go through high school drug-free and alcohol-free! The "trickle up" theory means that by the time the junior high kids are in high school the power of the SADD concepts will follow them and protect them.

The Tenets of the Junior High Program

The junior high program offers a new set of standards for children and parents to follow. The main points of this SADD program are these:

1. The kids promise to remain drug-free and alcohol-free. (Since most of them are already, they are not being asked to modify their behavior. All that is being asked is that they *continue* as they are.)

2. The kids promise to learn about drugs, their effects and consequences, and they agree to ask for information when they have questions about such matters.

3. The kids promise to talk with their parents about the issues of drugs and alcohol and other adolescent pressures such as smoking cigarettes, sex and dating.

4. The parents vow to talk about these topics openly with their children. In many cases parents themselves are ignorant about drugs and their effects, and other adolescent pressures. Parents and children must work together to educate each other.

5. Parents vow to be open to discussions about their child's intimate world. This is important to prevent the kind of closing off of the family that is so common among teenagers and parents.

These five simple steps can make a world of difference when your children reach high school. The burdens of those years will have been removed by the foundation of communication and trust that you have maintained within your own family.

Maintaining Parental Authority

Many parents fear that they relinquish their authority by becoming open to the things of which they disapprove. They fear that if they acknowledge the existence of alcohol and drugs and sex it means that their objections to them will be somehow diminished.

Phooey!

Kids need and want guidance and discipline. They need rules to protect them and assure them of our love and concern, but they also need to feel that those rules are personal. They want to know that your beliefs and expectations are what is best for them. They don't want to feel that you are advocating some rule that could apply to anyone, or that you impose on them because of what you fear the neighbors will think. They don't want rules designed to keep them out of your hair.

Kids want rules, but they want rules that come from your heart, and from your knowledge of them individually; they want to trust that you are advising them on their own best interests, that you know what *they* feel.

You lose authority by shutting out your kids. You strengthen authority by listening to their belief that they are special because they are who they are. Then the SADD motto—"I'm special because I'm me"—will have real impact on their lives.

None of us, parents, teachers or relatives, should have to wipe away our children's tears because they have lost a friend or classmate. *If* we can make the junior high program effective, *if* we can teach our younger kids how precious they are, I won't have to follow death across the country. You won't have to mourn. We can eliminate the drunk driving issue completely. We can be free to move on to the primary issue of drinking and taking drugs.

95

"We can't wait, Mr. A."

I received a letter from the younger sister of a SADD member. This girl, just entering junior high school, had watched her older brother struggle with the burdens of high school. She had heard her parents fight for control and she had seen it slipping away. And then she had seen how SADD had opened the family up and brought it together. She wanted the same chance. She was the first indication I had that these younger kids were watching and waiting for their chance to become involved in SADD.

The SADD Junior High School Curriculum

We have a formal outline of the SADD program for the junior high schools. It defines the basic goals as being:

1. To alert junior high students to the dangers of drugs and alcohol.

2. To conduct community drug and alcohol awareness programs through parent- and citizen-based workshops.

3. To assist in organizing peer counseling programs with local high school SADD members in order to assist junior high students who may have concerns about the use of drugs and alcohol.

To implement these goals, we believe that the use of a three-step approach, *School, Home* and *Community,* provides the best support system for a developing child.

Step One: The schools should provide support through the implementation of a SADD curriculum in a regular classroom situation and the establishment of an official SADD junior chapter.

Step Two: Family members should reinforce the school's efforts by reading, discussing and signing the Junior High Contract for Life (see page 97). Furthermore, they should read and discuss the official SADD booklets entitled: "Bob Anastas Talks to Parents" and "Let's Talk About Drugs and Alcohol."

CONTRACT
FOR
LIFE

JUNIOR HIGH SCHOOL SADD
A Contract for Life Between Parent and
Junior High Student

Junior High Student: I agree to learn as much as possible about the effects of illegal substances, to share with you my concerns about peer pressure and to discuss these issues openly with you. I will contact you immediately for advice and guidance if I ever find myself in a situation where illegal substances are present. Under this contract I make a commitment to you not to use illegal substances. I also agree that I will not accept a ride with anyone who has been under the influence of drugs or alcohol.

_____
Signature

Parent: I will seek information and educate myself about the realities of illegal substances. I agree to be an ever available resource for advice and communication with you. I agree that I will not use illegal substances. I also agree to seek safe, sober transportation home if I am ever in a situation where I have had too much to drink or a friend who is driving me has had too much to drink.

_____
Signature

_____
Date

S.A.D.D. does not condone drinking by those below the legal drinking age. S.A.D.D. encourages all young people to obey the laws of their state, including the laws relating to the legal drinking age.

Distributed by S.A.D.D., "Students Against Driving Drunk"

®

97

Step Three: The community should be brought into the organization through the active pursuit of local businesses and organizations to provide resources and support for SADD. The community can assist in projects by providing the opportunity to air public service announcements on local TV and radio, and funding the production and distribution of leaflets and posters. The participation of local law enforcement agencies in SADD awareness campaigns should also be pursued.

The College and University
SADD Movement

The same excitement that surrounds the beginning of the SADD junior high programs is evident on our college and university campuses across the country. The young men and women who have gone out to make their futures know that there is a lot at stake, and they want to succeed. They want to be taken seriously. Many of this year's college students participated in SADD in high school; they understand and appreciate its principles and now they have a chance to continue their commitment.

Drinking and drugs are a reality on college campuses that we cannot deny or ignore. Testimony given before the President's Commission on Drunk Driving by college administrators cited alcohol use as the leading cause of academic failure. The advent of higher legal drinking ages in many states has made campuses legally dry, but the law is too easily broken.

Young adults need support, too. The college administration, their community, their peers and family are still essential to their well-being. Our main goal is to work together to make these young adults appreciate their special position in the world.

They are the future. There is tremendous power and pride in that undeniable fact; all young people want to fulfill their ambitions and dreams. It is that sense of expansive hope and energy that SADD taps to implement this program.

Parents of college students have a less active role to play in the ongoing structure of SADD, but their role is still important. Not only can parents contact the administration, through the dean of students, to suggest that they look into forming a SADD group, parents can offer young adults the same interest, advice and chance for communication that is so important to kids in the younger groups. Communication should not stop when children leave home; they still need their parents' wisdom and love. Sometimes their world may be overwhelming, and finding a way into a teenager's intimate circle may be more challenging. Parents must tell their kids how they feel, and ask them questions about their lives. The results are worth it.

The rest of this section is addressed to college and university students. It should help you translate your experience with SADD from high school to the campus. It will show you how to get your new community involved.

We recognize that you are surrounded by drugs and alcohol, and that you must deal with that reality. We recognize that you may not be able to deal with it alone—that's just too hard.

On a campus you have a whole new community, and none of your old support systems. You have new friends. You do not have the daily presence of your parents.

All of you must forge a caring and supportive community. You each need to know you can rely on your peers for help. SADD is an effective way to form this community of care.

The basic goals of the SADD university and college program are:

1. To help eliminate the drunk driver and save lives.

2. To promote responsible behavior by college students by not mixing driving with drugs or alcohol.

3. To reduce the alcohol-related deaths, injuries and arrests in college communities.

4. To encourage responsible use of alcoholic beverages by students of legal age who choose to drink.

5. To demonstrate that the majority of college students are responsible adults with a genuine concern for alleviating drunk driving.

In order to begin a SADD chapter on your campus, follow these seven steps:

1. Meet with a faculty advisor or dean of students as well as other student organization representatives to explain the goals of SADD.

2. Choose a faculty member who can serve as an advisor and as a liaison between you and the administration.

3. Elect SADD officers.

4. Obtain or produce your own information on drugs and alcohol for distribution on campus.

5. Plan a calendar of SADD activities.

6. Reach out to the community at large to get the support of local businesses and organizations for SADD projects.

7. Contact the national SADD office for an official certificate and to obtain advice and help if needed. We will be glad to provide speakers to launch your efforts.

Once you have done the necessary groundwork you can turn your attention to the campus at large. Your campus is filled with organizations that can all participate in spreading the SADD message; you and your fellow SADD members want to introduce the concepts to as many different groups of students and organizations as possible. The Greek organizations can sponsor a SADD awareness campaign around homecoming time. The student athletic association can distribute SADD literature at its intramural games. The school paper may want to feature a series of articles on the effects of drinking and driving. The debate society may choose to conduct a debate around the issue of taking drugs.

Consider these possible activities:

1. Sponsor a SADD Awareness Week. You can set up tables for distribution of educational material on drinking, drugs and driving in the library or student union.

2. Publish a regular SADD newsletter that highlights SADD meetings, activities and news from chapters on other campuses.

3. Produce radio and TV announcements addressing the drunk driving issue.

CONTRACT FOR LIFE

THE COLLEGE CONTRACT FOR LIFE
BETWEEN FRIENDS

As students at _____, we recognize that many of our fellow students and friends choose to use alcoholic beverages and, that on occasion, some students may find themselves in a potential DWI situation.

Therefore, we have entered into a contract in which we agree that if we are ever in a situation where we have had too much to drink, or a friend or date who has had too much to drink, we will seek safe and sober transportation home.

We, the undersigned, also agree that we will provide or arrange safe, sober transportation home for each other should either of us face a situation where we have had too much to drink.

If we cannot find safe transportation, we will contact a taxi service, walk or stay the night.

_____   _____
Signature of 1st Party   Signature of 2nd Party

_____
Date

®

4. Establish auxiliary programs such as "the buddy system," developed by Anheuser Busch, that are designed to encourage college-age friends to watch over one another when they are at parties.

5. Establish a SADD center that carries all SADD merchandise items and free literature.

6. Conduct training programs for all employees of campus area bars and fraternity, sorority and dorm leaders on responsibly serving alcoholic beverages.

7. Acquire the drug and alcohol awareness materials available from local law enforcement officials and citizen groups.

You want the campus and the community to understand the importance of this issue. Frankly, many towns are not crazy about the local college kids. They feel threatened by the wild parties and rowdy behavior of a minority of students. You, through SADD, have a chance to repair this rift. We urge you to expand your SADD activities to involve the community and inform them of your campus's commitment to responsible conduct among students.

Consider, too, these options:

1. Sponsoring a SADD booth at a local shopping center during Alcohol Awareness Week on campus. Distribute material and sell SADD merchandise to raise money for your chapter.

2. Booking appearances by SADD members on local radio and TV talk shows to spread the word.

3. Working with the local police and citizen groups to sponsor public service announcements for airing on local media.

4. Putting up SADD posters in high visibility areas around town.

5. Getting a local or state political figure involved in one of your large on-campus SADD activities. Make that person the honorary chairman of your chapter. Contact media to get press coverage.

Both the junior high and university chapters offer our young people a chance to participate in the SADD idea for all their teenage years. One day, if we all work together, we may find that we no longer have to fight back the evils of drug and alcohol abuse. Our children will have gone through life with the support and information they need to choose the best life they can!

FOUR

Take Charge

I am doing all I can. The kids are doing a great job of spreading the SADD message. Now it is up to the rest of you: families, schools and communities who have not yet uncovered your potential for care.

—Robert Anastas

** 10 **

Coming Together

None of us can fight our battles alone. Even the wisest and the strongest of us need support and assistance from those who make up our personal circle. I firmly believe that each child needs a network of three important support systems: the family, the schools, and the community.

When all three systems work to help young people grow strong and secure they are in great shape to face life's adversities. If any one is not a part of their support system then they must increase our reliance on the remaining two. If they have a shortage of support from any two, then they are hard pressed to fight our battles effectively. If, heaven forbid, three are missing, they have a gargantuan struggle ahead.

SADD is designed to bring all three systems into line, to offer our kids the best chance for a healthy, happy life.

All individuals grow up in a network of environments that shape their character, for good or bad. The family, the schools

FORCES INFLUENCING INDIVIDUAL'S SENSE OF SELF

IMPACT ON INDIVIDUAL FROM VALUES

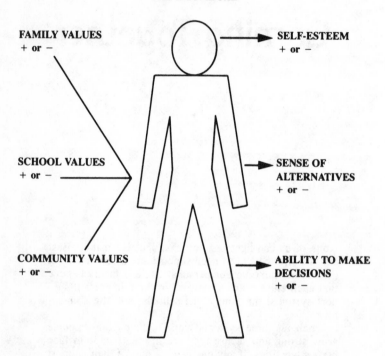

THE INDIVIDUAL

FAMILY VALUES
+ or −

SELF-ESTEEM
+ or −

SCHOOL VALUES
+ or −

SENSE OF ALTERNATIVES
+ or −

COMMUNITY VALUES
+ or −

ABILITY TO MAKE DECISIONS
+ or −

WHEN FAMILY, SCHOOL AND COMMUNITY GIVE POSITIVE VALUES THE RESULTS ARE POSITIVE SELF-ESTEEM, A POSITIVE SENSE OF ALTERNATIVES AND A POSITIVE ABILITY TO MAKE DECISIONS.

SADD IS DEDICATED TO MAKING IT POSSIBLE FOR THE FAMILY, SCHOOLS AND COMMUNITY TO MAKE A POSITIVE CONTRIBUTION TO THE FORMATION OF THE VALUES OF OUR YOUNG PEOPLE.

and the community at large all are influences that affect our sense of personal worth, our personal ethics and our behavior.

The family, schools and community all offer guidelines about what we should or shouldn't do, about what we should or shouldn't think about right and wrong, and about what are our responsibilities to ourselves and others. These guidelines all act together to influence each individual's basic values.

These values, both positive and negative, have a great impact on our personal happiness and success. In the best of all possible worlds, these three systems work together to give each person a positive foundation for becoming a healthy individual. But when one or more of these support systems is lacking, then, with luck, the others can take up the slack. The reason I want kids to take responsibility for themselves, for families to open up communication, for schools to institute the SADD curriculum and for communities to work to abolish teenage drinking and drinking and driving, is to give kids positive support from all their environmental influences.

Values is a word that describes the essential ethics we live by.

Our family may communicate values such as hard work, love and honesty, or it may seem to imply that toughness, competition and lack of emotional expressiveness are virtues.

Our schools may instill a value for hard work and self-improvement, or may simply provide a custodial service.

Our community may give us values such as service to other people, or values such as manipulation or apathy.

We each have a choice about how we live our lives, and we each have a choice about how our family, the schools and the community impact on us and our children.

We can strengthen the values that our children learn, not just at home, but from society. We can make those support systems positive influences.

Whether we make a difference depends on how we recognize and transmit our values. To be effective two basic techniques are required:

Communication is how we share our ideas and opinions with

others. It is essential to clarifying our values and seeing them take root.

If we cannot talk to one another in the family or at school meetings or within our community then we will all flounder. Not only will our young people become victims of negative peer pressure, but we will lose the joy of family life and our own sense of esteem.

Alternatives and choices are opened up by communicating our problems and questions. We each, as isolated individuals, can get stuck if we cannot see alternatives to our behavior and feelings. If your children feel peer pressure to drink or do drugs they will be hard pressed to resist if you have not helped them discover alternatives.

We have to help our kids. We have to help ourselves. We have to let our kids grow so they can be responsible for themselves. The welfare of all of us depends on the welfare of each of us.

I am confronted with this simple truth week after week as I travel across the country.

I see kids, good kids, who lack support and guidance from one or more of the basic support systems. In Oregon, for example, after I'd given my speech to a group of kids at Medford High School, one young girl stood up and said, "I've lost my mother. Dad is an alcoholic. I don't want to lose him. If he wrinkles up the contract, and throws it away, you know what I'm going to do? I'm going to unwrinkle the contract every time he throws it away, until I get him to sign it!"

The entire assembly fell silent and then broke into applause. I felt so much for that girl. She was so brave. Thank God she was not alone!

My answer to her and to kids all over the country is: You have four good support systems available.

You have yourself.

Hey, don't laugh; there is great power in *you*. You have the chance to be strong, to make a difference in your life, to make choices. Every time you run from the pressures of your life, every time you get high or drunk, you've made a choice, a negative choice. You can just as well make a positive one. You are responsible for yourselves. You aren't anyone's puppet, not if you don't want to be. But while you must take responsibility for yourself, you can look to others for support, too.

Second, you do have your fellow classmates. You may not know everyone in your school. You may not even like some of the ones you know, but which of you would wish each other bad fortune? You are all in this together; you have to live together every day. How you live together is up to you, but you each know in your hearts that you'd like to live happy, not unhappy. You'd like to live with hope, not despair. You'd like to grow up, get out of school and make the life you dream about come true.

So, pull together. Together you can shape your futures; if you are isolated you will only hurt yourselves. There's a lot of spirit and brain power in every school; no one can stop it if it is put to good ends.

You and your classmates can be your community.

And remember, you have me. I have traveled a thousand miles, in order to stand up in front of you and pour my guts out. I have told you about all the pain in my life. I am here to tell you that I won't let you die; I won't let you feel alone or uncared for. I won't stand for it and you shouldn't either.

I have told you about Buddy and John. You've had friends who have died. They gave their lives for all of us, and I won't have any of us turn our backs on their sacrifice.

Last of all, you have SADD. You have an international network of loyal friends who are working to keep you alive, and happy.

I have complete faith in the young people of our world. Kids can find self-esteem and personal responsibility; we parents and teachers can, too. Together, we can forge a better life for each of us.

111

11

Home Improvements

Talk. Listen. Ask questions.

Three simple acts of life that make all the difference. You kids aren't talking to your parents. You rarely listen. And you never ask questions.

Moms and Dads, I know that you haven't had a real talk with your children in a long time either. You don't want to listen to what they say if it's disagreeable to you. You probably do ask questions, but you don't want to hear the answers if they are upsetting.

Truce time! We have got to agree to make peace. We have got to agree that the family is the best place to go for love and guidance. Then we have to agree to work, and I mean work, to make that the case.

You spend hours weeding the lawn, fixing the roof, redoing the kitchen. Your inner home, the family, is just as important. So let's begin.

A Word to the Kids

I want you to know that my love for you and your love for me is strong enough to keep you from ever being trapped in a situation that may hurt you or may jeopardize your life.

Believe me, and believe that such love is there between you and your family as well. It may not be perfect love. It may be full of complications. "We've got problems in our family," my son Willy reminds me all the time. "We are not the Brady Bunch of the eighties!"

We all have problems. Some of you have parents who are divorced. Some of you have parents who don't get along well themselves. Some of you feel so much like strangers in your own house that you can't imagine having an open relationship with your folks. But even in those families, there is a bond of love that is stronger than the challenges of death, and you, if you are smart and responsible, can enjoy its fruits. Don't make the mistake of turning your home into a hotel where you just hang your hat, sleep and go.

You have to examine what you've done in the past few years to change your relationship to your parents. As a child your mom and dad were your best friends and they provided your most intimate relationships. But now, as a senior at a Boston high school put it, "I'm not about to tell my father what it's like at the parties I go to. He'd ground me just for going."

Why?

Think about it: You have shut your folks out of your world completely. Then, one day, you tell them what's really going on; it hits them like a bombshell. No wonder they react dramatically! But if you keep them informed, a little bit at a time, by discussing the pressures and realities of your life, then they won't be scared or upset when you go to them with a problem. They'll understand your world, they'll know what your personal conflicts and troubles are, and they will help you better prepare to handle them, not to submit to them.

You and your folks must *build* trust. Your parents can't bestow it on you; you have to work with them to let trust grow. If you look at it as a process of mutual education—they find out about you, you find out about them—then it is not so unimaginable that you might tell them what went on at some party you attended. You won't scare them to death, and you won't fear their reactions.

But what if you've been systematically protecting them from your reality for years? What if you are a senior who hasn't told them a thing since you entered high school? They probably believe you've never even seen an open bottle of beer, don't have friends who have done drugs and never have had to deal with your sexuality.

Well, the Contract for Life exists to help you break the ice.

The Contract (see page 115) is designed to get you and your folks together. It is a discussion starter. It acknowledges that teenage drinking exists in the world and teenage drinking and driving exists. It does not say that *you* are drinking or thinking of drinking and driving; it says that you want their help. It says you want to be protected from the terrible consequences of drinking, and drinking and driving. You are telling them that you need their trust, love and help to get through your teenage years. It is nothing short of a contract of love, and offering it to your parents is a way to say, "I love you and I want your help, if I ever need it."

The contract is also a way for you to tell your parents that you too have an active love for them, for it asks them to let *you* help them if they ever need assistance to manage a drinking, or drinking and driving situation.

The contract says quite clearly that once either of you has reached out and helped the other to avoid challenging death, you will discuss the problems.

The first step in improving your relationship with your parents is to talk, listen and ask questions. The other important step is to bring home the Contract for Life for discussion. You will find the rewards enormous, but it isn't necessarily easy.

CONTRACT
FOR
LIFE

A Contract for Life
Between Parent and Teenager
The SADD Drinking-Driver Contract

Teenager   I agree to call you for advice and/or transportation at any hour, from any place, if I am ever in a situation where I have been drinking or a friend or date who is driving me has been drinking.

_____
Signature

Parent   I agree to come and get you at any hour, any place, no questions asked and no argument at that time, or I will pay for a taxi to bring you home safely. I expect we would discuss this issue at a later time.

I agree to seek safe, sober transportation home if I am ever in a situation where I have had too much to drink or a friend who is driving me has had too much to drink.

_____
Signature

_____
Date

S.A.D.D. does not condone drinking by those below the legal drinking age. S.A.D.D. encourages all young people to obey the laws of their state, including laws relating to the legal drinking age.

Distributed by S.A.D.D., "Students Against Driving Drunk"

®

115

THE CONTRACT FOR LIFE

Most of your parents will sign this contract, because what
we're asking them to do is keep you alive and talk about a
solution to this problem when you get home. But there are
some of you that will bring the contract home and have it
ripped up and probably thrown right in your face.

What your father and mother are saying to you is, "SADD? I
don't want to play that game. I'm afraid of what's happening in
your world. Maybe it will go away."

If that happens you must not despair or turn away from the
SADD program. You must continue to work with your classmates and your teachers, your community and, yes, your
parents. You have a responsibility, too, for the breakdown in
communication between you and your parents. Even when
they block your efforts to get the contract signed you must try
to make them understand and keep up communication.

Understanding Your Parents' Fears

Just as you are ultimately responsible for how you conduct
yourself, for drinking, drinking and driving, or taking drugs,
you are responsible for your relationship with your parents.
They are not only parents, they are people too. This may come
as a shock to you, but they have feelings, confusions and fears
like anybody else. You need to understand their emotions, just
as you want them to understand yours.

One of the things parents fear most is the loss of their
authority. If they are opposed to your point of view on an issue
they don't want to have to be a rubber stamp for behavior they
don't believe in to keep peace in the house. They don't want to
be put in a position where you throw your rebellion or disagreement in their face. No human being on earth wants their
beliefs mocked. You sure don't. So why should they?

Communication is not a one-way street. Their job is not for
them to listen passively to what you have to say, you must
both *actively* listen to each other.

You must understand the simple truth that they have lived
longer than you, seen more, and been through a lot more than

116

you imagine. They have formed a belief system that they value. You may disagree with it but you have no right to dismiss it. They are motivated by love for you, by the desire to protect you from the harshness of life. Don't forget it.

When you present your world to them, do not do so as a challenge. That is as stupid as challenging death by drinking and driving.

People who have mutual trust must acknowledge that when they disagree they still maintain respect for one another. That means that you must retain respect for your parents even when you think their perspectives are "square."

All of this may seem a little hard to swallow until you look at it this way: Your life is in danger, actually in danger, if you don't have the trust, support and love of family, school and community. Most important of these groups is your family. You may think it's a hassle to listen to and respect your parents but the alternative is grimmer. It is a life lived alone.

If you are grown up enough to want to make your own decisions then you must be grown up enough to understand that sometimes others have their own wisdom, even when you disagree with it.

Don't get impatient; it's not easy for anyone to keep communication open in a family, but it's worth the trouble. And I'm going to tell your parents the same thing.

Thoughts for Parents

What has happened to the world?

I don't know. Sometimes it looks like it's gone mad. I feel it as much as you do.

As an educator and a parent of three teenage boys, I understand your concerns about the use and abuse of alcohol and other drugs by our children. My experience has led me to believe that as determined as we are to provide a drug-free environment for our children, statistics have proven that our efforts to date have fallen on deaf ears.

This is not to say that we must not continue to work towards this end, but we must begin to react to the present reality. As our children grow away from us, we hear such things as: "Don't worry." "I know what I'm doing." "It's my business." "My world is different from yours." No wonder many of us are shocked when we find out that our children have been using illegal substances.

I meet parents all the time who live in a happy fantasy that their kids don't have to face pressure about alcohol and drugs. But that is a very fragile "happiness," for what you don't know can hurt you!

Through the process of parenting, mothers and fathers have worked at building up, over the years, a great deal of trust and respect with their children. They do this by using love, and sometimes fear. Children also wish to please their parents for many reasons. They will tell them repeatedly that they are living a clean, healthful life where no drugs are allowed and where people who are doing drugs are not part of their life. They want their parents to believe this.

Folks, there are three realities in your children's lives that we wish would go away: drinking, drugs and sex. We don't like them. In a perfect world we could say "don't drink or do drugs," and kids wouldn't. But we don't live in a perfect world. All we can do is make a start by educating ourselves about alcohol and drugs and sex.

Once we have done our homework, we must find constructive ways of showing our children we care. Then we can begin to work together as a family to make communication an everyday event.

The SADD Contract for Life is the first step in creating a safeguard against death. I believe you want your children to realize that they can and should call you if they are ever faced with a drinking-driving situation; both you and I know that this does not condone the illegal use of alcohol on their part. It does, however, show that your love for your children and their love for you is strong enough to combat any obstacle that may force them to challenge death.

You must educate yourselves about drugs and alcohol. Over

and over, kids tell me they walk through their homes, stoned out of their minds, and their parents never notice! The kids take this as a sign of indifference, though more often it is simply a sign of ignorance. Parents don't know what to look for. They are unaware of the signals that are given to them.

We cannot cling to our ignorance. We must be brave enough as parents to face the unpleasant truths of life.

Talia Ofek, the 1985 president of the Syosset, Long Island, SADD chapter was invited to bring her school's improvisational theater group to a meeting of the local Republican Club. The theater group presented a very forceful drama/discussion program about the issues of drug and alcohol use by local teenagers. One woman in particular was concerned after the show. "How can you imply that our kids are affected by these traumas?" she demanded. "They don't drink. They don't do drugs. They don't have these problems."

The kids were not surprised by the reaction. They have seen it over and over. Parents who hope that the world is one way refuse to acknowledge the realities that face their children.

To help you learn about these problems I have included a brief outline of the signs and effects of drug use and a drug awareness test in Appendix B, pages 143-48. Even if your children are drug-free you should be aware of the signals. Your children must deal with the problem of friends, classmates or acquaintances who use alcohol and drugs. If you are uneducated and unaware, your children will be reluctant to ask your advice about handling whatever situation they encounter.

Joint Efforts

Now is the time to bring you parents and children together. You both have acknowledged enough interest in the issues surrounding family communication to read this far—don't stop now. The hard work and the glorious rewards are right around the corner.

No matter how difficult it is at first to get communication going again in your family, remember the alternatives.

How many of you parents and kids have played the following scene, over and over again. Your son or daughter walks up to you and says, "Daddy, may I have the car keys?" You reply, "Sure. But where are you going?" Your child replies simply, "Out." Isn't that great? "We have a full tank of gas," you say. "And I'd like you home by eleven." So your child reassures you: "Daddy, no problem." You add, "I don't want you to do the following: Don't drive fast. Don't go to any strange parties. Don't go with people I wouldn't approve of. Don't you dare drink. I know you don't, but just in case. If there's booze at the party, you leave. And whatever you do, don't get into any car with anyone who has been drinking and don't you dare drive under the influence."

Well, eleven o'clock rolls around. You hear the car pull in. "Say, this isn't bad," you think. "He's here!" But before your child goes to bed, you slip out and check the odometer. Four hundred miles! Your child left at eight and came in at eleven. There aren't four hundred miles in the town. So, you approach your kid as any parent should and ask, "Where have you been?" The response? "No place." "Who were you with?" "No one." "Did you have fun?" "I had a ball!" Now, wait a minute! If you put that little conversation together . . . he has been no place with no one and he's having a hysterical time, then the best part of the conversation is to follow.

"Have you been drinking?" you demand. "Drinking?" he repeats. "Was there any liquor at the party?" "Liquor at the party?" "Were there any friends there I wouldn't approve of?" "Friends you wouldn't approve of?" Are you raising a parrot? So you say, "Go to bed." He goes upstairs to his room, lies in his bed and says, "Ho, ho, it's getting close but I put it over on him! He doesn't know anything! I talk to him but he doesn't know anything." His father is saying, "I don't know what, but that kid's doing something. But then again he did talk to me," but *you* know he didn't say anything. You love your child. You want to trust him. But when you have moved outside his intimate circle, when you don't have that close communication that you want, you get evasive answers to any direct questions you ask about his private life.

And what happens when *your* kids have a party at *your* house?

Do you leave your home for a weekend, knowing full well that your teenage kids will have a party? Do you pretend there's no harm in it? Do you refuse to accept your responsibilities to act as an active host to the kids who come to your house?

The number of parents who do refuse would astonish you.

Sure, you would like to think that your kids are angels who would never do anything of which you'd disapprove, but face it, they've got a lot of pressures to handle: from their friends, from uninvited guests who force their rowdy lifestyle on your kids, from their own inclination to try and get away with as much as possible.

If you were there, they would not have to face those pressures alone.

You owe them that.

The SADD Guide to Teenage Parties outlines the basic steps you can take to make your kids' parties safe; it is a way of proving that you care what happens to them. See Appendix C (page 149).

Wanting to believe that your child is still as open and innocent with you as he was in the lower grades will not change reality. It will not roll back the death statistics from drinking, drugs or suicide. Only the hard and rewarding work of getting the family together and talking openly can accomplish that.

There are four basic ways you and your family can work together to begin opening up the lines of communication:
1. scheduling regular family meetings,
2. participating in values clarification,
3. signing the Contract for Life,
4. sharing information and awareness tests together.

These steps may seem somewhat formal or stiff, but in the beginning when everyone is a little nervous about talking to each other it helps if you can plan a formal agenda.

Before you begin any of these meetings, however, you and

your kids must both make a formal agreement: You must promise not to interrupt each other, to give each other a fair hearing, and to try not to jump to conclusions. Sentences like, "Dad, you never hear what I'm saying," or "Son, what I say is the rule," won't get you anywhere.

• Family meetings

Either children or parents can ask for a family meeting. Don't hesitate to initiate it; simply say that you are interested in improving your communication and want to set aside a special time, without other distractions, so that everyone can share thoughts and feelings.

Once the first meeting has been held you can try and set a loose schedule so that you meet regularly.

There is no set topic for the first meeting unless you want to address a special issue. If you wish, any of you can introduce the Contract for Life or set up a value clarification session.

• Value clarification

This is a method of checking out each other's beliefs through hypothetical situations, and investigating potential trouble before it occurs. Parents and children discuss "what if"; the point is to find out *ahead of time* what each of you would do if confronted with a difficult situation. If your child has been out drinking with friends and comes home high, that is no time to explore each other's beliefs.

Remember that this should be done with good will, patience and understanding. It is not a format for a fight, but a way to gently explore each other's opinions and feelings.

For example, a teenager may want to ask his/her parents:

"If I were to throw a party and kids came with beer, what would you do?"

Once they answer, the teenager wants to further probe his/her parents' feelings by asking:

"Why would you do that?"

Then the teenager should tell his/her parents what he would like them to do. If they have a conflict then they must explore a way to establish an agreement that will work.

Parents may want to pose a hypothetical situation to their child, such as:

"If you are ever in a party situation with other kids who are drinking, what would you do?"

Remember, this is hypothetical, no one is admitting guilt. No one is asking to get punished for his or her reactions. The family is opening up a whole world of new topics for discussion so that parents and children can find out how they each might react to tough life situations.

If a child says that he would probably have a drink if he was in that hypothetical party situation, parents have a chance to explain why they do not think that is the best choice. They have a chance to express their opinions and their care.

Value clarification is a method that can be applied to *any* topic of discussion: drugs, school work, sex, politics, dress, drinking, treatment of siblings, you name it. The key is to keep the tough questions hypothetical. The goal is to exchange intimate information about your beliefs and the reasons for those beliefs.

One way to make sure that both parents and children are aware of the effects of alcohol is to bring an awareness quiz to the scheduled discussion. This quiz can be done together, or one of you can ask the others for their answers. The quiz is also a great starting point for discussion of general life issues. It can be found in Appendix D, page 151.

When you begin to improve your family communication skills, you should examine the way you talk to your children. It is often as important *how* you talk to one another as *what* you say. Here are some further suggestions:

• Maintain a consistent set of rules and standards. Almost all psychologists have determined that the stability and happiness of a child depends on consistent, predictable enforcement of rules and standards. Children need to know that what is acceptable one day will be so the next; conversely, they need to believe that what is unacceptable one time will not be overlooked the next. If you are consistent, then your children will respect your standards and credibility, even if they disagree with them.

- Keep your promises—and don't make promises you can't keep. The easiest way to lose your child's respect is to say you will do something and then fail to come through. Remember, your children want to respect you. Let them.
- Don't always be disapproving or sarcastic. Children who find that they are ridiculed for everything they say soon will stop saying anything! Children want and need acceptance.
- Don't preach or moralize. Don't deliver a sermon every time your children do something wrong. Enforce your rules consistently; make your point of view known; listen to your child's response. This allows you to work together in the future to prevent the same disagreements from arising. Preaching only keeps your children from really listening to what you are saying.

A family is a precious unit, but it is not our only resource. Both parents and children can work with their schools and community to keep a caring dialogue alive. Kids can plan meetings for their parents that provide accurate information about the tough realities of teenage drug and alcohol use in their school. Parents can work with the administration to have educational curriculum about drugs and alcohol in the classroom and can help plan lectures by experts in the field.

Let's look at the next two chapters to see the wide variety of activities that you can do and that are already being done by parents and students across the country.

** 12 **

In the Schools

The school today is a source of enormous impact on children and their families. Too often, however, the impact is harmful. Students are burdened by negative peer pressure; parents feel alienated from the main activity of their children. This is unnecessary. Students, parents and teachers, working separately or together, can change the impact of the school by creating caring programs that keep communication open, and our kids safe.

I have always believed that the kids of this country were ready and able to lead us in this area. I have proven this through SADD—they have the imagination and drive to make a difference. Our SADD chapter projects have sprung up all over motivated by kids-helping-kids. In this chapter we will look first at what these innovative students are doing before we explore alternatives for parents and for faculty.

A Word to the Kids

You are in a position to be leaders. You know what's going on in your world. You know who is in trouble in your school with alcohol or drugs. You know that the statistics (there are 3.3 million teenage alcoholics in this country) are true. You know how badly you feel about the pressures in your life.

You hold the key to change.

Starting a SADD Chapter

It is easy to start a SADD chapter. We can provide you with a starter kit and arrange for a SADD speaker to appear at your school. All you have to do is:

1. Post a notice of an after-school meeting in order to gather interested students.

2. Once a core group has assembled you can approach a teacher or counselor in your school to accept the position of faculty advisor.

3. Working with the faculty advisor you can schedule regular meetings and plan informational campaigns.

4. Once the faculty advisor and basic core group are established you can write to SADD headquarters for an official membership.

That's it!

Now you are ready to begin your SADD activities. The first step is almost always to obtain permission to establish a SADD day at the school. For this day you blanket the halls with SADD posters (from our starter kit) and set up a booth in the lobby or lunchroom that has SADD literature, copies of the contract and SADD merchandise, such as key rings and bumper stickers, available for sale.

You and your faculty advisor might also wish to have a SADD spokesperson or a local expert in drug and alcohol issues or law enforcement speak to a school assembly. This is a way to get the facts out as quickly as possible.

After this SADD day you will want to increase your membership drive. Furthermore, it is important to establish a regular calendar of events. Every month you want to schedule some activity that will keep the SADD message in the minds of your fellow students.

Suggested SADD Chapter Activities

Place SADD materials and posters at liquor stores or anywhere alcohol is sold.

Have SADD awareness campaigns before all proms, homecomings, graduation, Senior Week, holidays, etc.

Place SADD reminders in the pockets of rental tuxedos.

For parades such as Homecoming or Labor Day, enter a SADD Float.

Take out ads in your local newspaper with a SADD message or slogans.

Present the SADD program to area junior high schools and elementary schools.

Have a SADD Safe Summer Campaign using billboards and other means to advertise. Solicit all parents to sponsor and support SADD. Get them involved.

Make SADD public service announcements for radio.

Stage a mock Driving While Intoxicated (DWI) arrest, trial and conviction using real judges, lawyers, police and students.

Arrange buses for transportation to events such as proms and parties, and encourage the use of limousines or taxi cab service.

Work with parents to set up a weekend hot-line service, for kids to call if they are incapable of driving and need a ride home.

As you can see, there is no end to the activities you students can initiate. SADD is your organization, it lives on your energy and imagination. However, it also depends on the cooperation and help of your faculty advisor.

A Word to the School Administration and Teachers

Once students have taken the initiative to start a SADD chapter the faculty advisor plays a vital role. She or he is a key to shaping the focus of activities and keeping the energy and interest high. If you are interested in being a faculty advisor yourself, or if as a parent or student, you want to involve a local school representative, it is important to understand the role of the faculty advisor.

According to one faculty advisor to SADD, "The kids come to me for advice or information about how to approach community leaders, or local businesses to get them involved with SADD. They also depend on me to keep the urgency of the SADD message fresh in the minds of the other faculty and administration. These kids are my friends. I offer constant encouragement and reaffirmation for their work."

"We have a wonderful faculty advisor," Kim Mussmann, member of the Longwood Chapter in 1985, explains, "because she is always available to any student who wants to discuss the kinds of problems SADD confronts. She helps us with the program but she also helps us with the issues that affect our lives." Kim, who has been active in her chapter for three years, feels that the team approach gives everyone the most strength needed to fight peer pressure and to get the support of parents, school administration and community. "With an active faculty advisor, there isn't anything we can't accomplish."

Advisors may choose to work with fellow teachers to integrate SADD into various classes or they may choose to institute it as a new program itself. The success of SADD rests heavily on the energy and enthusiasm of these dedicated advisors. We are always available to offer them any help they need. The kids, SADD, and I personally, all owe a debt of thanks to these fine educators across the country.

The faculty advisor is also a vital force in bringing the official SADD curriculum into the regular classroom. The SADD curriculum, available from our national office, is a basic outline of classroom instruction for teachers. It outlines not only the topics for discussion but offers suggested methods for involving the students and makes a variety of tapes and literature available for classroom use. It also guides you in tapping the expert advice of professional drug and alcohol counselors in your community. Please don't hesitate to send for your copy.

A Word to Parents

If you are interested in having your child's school begin a SADD chapter and implement the SADD curriculum, there are five ways to begin:

1. Make an appointment to go see the principal or student counselor. Bring a SADD curriculum and book or any SADD literature you have with you. Show them the program and set out your goals.

2. Speak to other parents whom you believe will support you. Organize a lobbying group.

3. Urge the school to conduct drug and alcohol awareness programs, with films and outside lecturers.

4. Contact the national SADD office to arrange for a speaker to conduct an assembly at your child's school.

5. Speak with your children about the program.

SADD is a student organization. You will never be in a position where you are running the chapter, but you can work *for* your kids to help persuade the school administration of the need for a chapter. And you can help the kids raise funds and get public attention by using your connection in the local business community to get projects off the ground.

Special SADD School Projects

The Michigan SADD organization, as we have seen in an earlier chapter, is particularly active. In 1985, 1,200 student representatives from over 1,000 high schools were brought together under the auspices of SADD for a statewide planning conference.

The students developed ideas for graduation week projects at each of their schools. Some of their ideas were:

• Organizing SADD awareness programs through distribution of informational literature.
• Running public service announcements on local radio and TV stations around graduation and prom weeks to get the "Friends don't let friends drive drunk" message across.

- Holding alternative parties that are drug-free and alcohol-free to celebrate graduation and proms.
- Beginning a SADD membership drive in April to build momentum through the end of school.
- Publishing a SADD newsletter to let all students know about the SADD message and to be aware of alternative activities that are available.
- Distributing the Contract for Life to get parents involved in the project.
- Holding a Senior Breakfast during graduation week. Give each senior a SADD memento.
- Plan a Dri-Hi Prom and Project Graduation for a safe and sober end to the school year. If you are interested in organizing a statewide drive for Project Graduation, have your SADD chapter faculty advisor contact the national SADD office or your local state Drug and Alcohol Education Office.

These are but a few of the various projects that have appeared all over the country as a result of the students' concern and interest in getting the SADD message across. I am constantly overwhelmed by the cleverness of the kids.* We started with a dream but it has become a 3-D technicolor extravaganza!

*There are several other student-run and motivated programs that address the problems of alcohol and drug use and abuse. For a list of these and their addresses see Appendix A on page 139.

✱✱ 13 ✱✱

Community Action

The community is the third vital link in the three-pronged attack on the problems facing our young people. The financial and moral support that local and national businesses and organizations have given the kids have made it possible for the SADD message to reach a national audience.

When kids learn how to work with and use the resources of the business community, they are well on the way to finding that they have far more power in the world at large than they ever imagined.

Just as I am proud to have our national organization supported by business contributions, I am proud that the local SADD chapters have worked with their local business community. Since that first SADD day in Wayland when the students were able to get Governor King involved, one of SADD's main missions is to show students how to use the power, money and energy of their local community.

There are many places students can go for assistance in their SADD public relations campaigns. The business community at large benefits economically from students' financial support. Small retailers, for example, depend on tuxedo rentals at prom time for their profits. Soft drink vendors, florists, local retail stores and restaurants and suppliers of athletic equipment have a business relationship with our young people. Additionally, local beer distributorships and retail liquor stores and taverns have an obligation, which they recognize and accept, to prevent underage people from obtaining liquor. Service organizations like men's clubs, women's groups, the Elks and Kiwanis are all set up to assist community concerns.

Even local media, which always want a good story, are open to the SADD message. Local radio shows welcome SADD chapter members for talk shows. Public service announcements are possible on radio, TV and in newspapers.

Some of the most popular and effective campaigns across the country have included billboards, car washes, literature distribution at retail liquor stores and production of public service announcements.

Billboards

Surry Central High School in Surry, North Carolina, was one of the first to arrange for billboards along their local roadways. North Merrick High School on Long Island, New York, has also done a similar campaign. In both instances, the local SADD chapter was able to obtain contributions for the painting supplies, printing costs, and rental of the billboards from local businesses. Working with the city governments and the state highway patrol, the members found the best location for the billboard and all the help they needed.

If you are interested in such an activity in your community, follow these steps:

1. Help your school conduct a school-wide contest to design

a SADD billboard. Offer suggested slogans such as "Friends Don't Let Friends Drive Drunk," or "If We Can Dream, We Can Make It So," or "Have a Safe and Sober Prom."

2. Help your school contact local businesspeople for contributions of money or supplies to produce the billboard.

3. Talk to local police and state patrol officers to get help in finding a good location. If an existing billboard is not available, obtain a permit to construct one.

4. Organize a group of students to put up or paint the billboard.

5. Contact local papers and radio stations to get them to run a story about the billboard and SADD.

Kim Mussman from North Merrick explains: "The best thing we did was put up the billboards on the road to the beach. During the summer, the SADD message was there every day, even though we weren't in school."

Your chapter can do the same.

Car Washes

Car washes are a reasonably easy and enjoyable way to raise money. A local shopping center may donate the space and water hook-ups for the day or a commercial car wash may allow you to use its facilities for a day. After costs, you can keep the profit. SADD pins, bumper stickers and T-shirts can be offered for sales. In all cases SADD literature is placed in the cars after washing and or after the merchandise is sold.

Literature Distribution

Contact local retail stores and places that sell beer and liquor, and ask if they will allow a SADD display and SADD pamphlets to be posted by the cash register. Many shops are glad to do this since it is a fine community service at no cost to them. Ask that they also make a small donation to your chapter or sell key rings and other merchandise for you. You can provide a collection jar for customers to pay into, so that the retailer does not have to keep track of the cash for you.

Ask local tuxedo retail shops and florists to place SADD

literature in their products at prom time. Another good project is to hang posters in high visibility areas, such as student hangouts.

Public Service Announcements

Your SADD group can record and produce PSAs for airing on local radio and TV. It's fun and it's also a very effective way to get your message across. Most radio stations will provide you with access to their recording facilities and help you package the material; all you need to do is to write and record the slogans. You may have a ten-second spot and a thirty-second spot. For TV, still photographs of the SADD logo or slogan may be used.

Local Government

Your local government can be an invaluable source of support. Almost all states have an office of youth education on drugs and alcohol, and many counties also have such programs. The state police are often active in such projects as well. Your state senator or representative will be glad to lend their support to your activities. You will be surprised at how many resources are available for the asking.

Some exciting projects have come about when statewide SADD conferences are held, inviting all of the state schools to participate. Dozens of states have held these conferences; most of them have been sponsored by Governors' Highway Safety Funds, local business and local or county governments in conjunction with organizations such as SADD.

These community activities, when combined with your home improvement program and school SADD chapter's activities assure your children of having the most secure and happy future possible.

The Best of Life Is Yet to Be

I have glimpsed the future, and I want to share that vision with you. It is not a dream. It is not a wish. It is a certainty if we will only continue, in the present, to help our kids help themselves.

Picture this. Your kids are growing up; they are no longer the dependent, sheltered childen you knew for the first decade of their lives. They are venturing out into the world, meeting all kinds of new and complicated situations.

But they are prepared.

They are not cut off from your support, advice and care.

They are not terrified of peer pressure.

They know they are special simply because they are themselves.

This doesn't mean there is never a fight in your house. We still have to battle and work to forge our good relationships, but the house feels different. You feel calmer. Your kids feel happier.

Why? Because you are facing the world together.

And the results?

Your kids don't feel *obliged* to go along with destructive peer pressure. In fact, it's hardly there. Those kids who advocate drugs and alcohol are an outcast minority who must deal with the positive peer pressure that tells them, "You are wrong."

We know that SADD and the kids have made a difference all over the country. There is a new mood. It is represented by the new higher drinking ages, by the increased enforcement of existing laws, by the fact that there is less drinking, and less drinking and driving.

Since 1981 SADD has grown from one chapter in Wayland to 8,000 in all fifty states, as well as Europe, Guam and Canada. We have three full-time speakers on staff. Every day SADD presentations are made; every week over 20,000 Contracts are distributed! But we aren't going to rest.

One day I hope that SADD can find the means to open a year-round camp that offers kids from all over the country a place to come with their parents for several weeks a year. There, they will be exposed to the finest teachers and lecturers on art, computers and other subjects, to give them creative outlets for their curious intellects and emotions. There, parents and kids will have a chance to spend intensive time in workshops learning to hone their communication skills.

If we have flourishing chapters for all age groups, and my dream of a camp comes true, we will have blanketed the country with our message of love and care. When I started this program the only question I had was "How in God's name could I get to the kids?" One person even said to me, "Bob, no way is it going to work. You can't mobilize kids across the country! You can't start a life-saving crusade against drinking, and drinking and driving, especially with teenagers." When I said, "Why?" he replied, "Because they're burn-outs. Because they don't care about each other." And I said, "What are you talking about? I have teenage sons. They have friends. They all care about what happens to each other."

My message to the kids is: If you believe the way I believe that you are powerful, then you can eliminate the killer facing you—in fact, you can eliminate *any* obstacle facing you. If you believe that you are powerful and that you can make a difference, then commit yourself to this program.

But if you procrastinate, and someone in your school dies in a drinking and driving accident, it's your burden, because you have the power to stop the slaughter. But if you start the SADD program and no one dies or gets hurt from drunk driving, you're going to have the greatest feeling you've ever had in your life.

I am giving you my seventeen-year-old son and saying to you, "Keep him alive." That's what all of us fathers and mothers are saying to you. We can't give you a more heartfelt testimony as to how much we believe in you. Please, please join with me, for the best of life is yet to be.

Resources

Here is a list of organizations that can offer you advice and support in managing your concerns about drinking and drug use and abuse. Many of these groups have models available for schools and organizations to set up chapters and projects in local communities. They also provide factual literature and can send speakers to your schools.

AAA Foundation for Traffic
  Safety
8111 Gatehouse Rd.
Falls Church, VA 22047
(703) 222-6891

Association of State and
  Territorial Health Officials
Suite 3A
1311A Dolly Madison Blvd.
McLean, VA 22101
(703) 556-9222

Bacchus of the United States,
  Inc.
Tigert Hall—Room 124
University of Florida
Gainesville, FL 32611
(904) 392-1261

Citizens for Safe Drivers
  Against Drunk Drivers
  & Chronic Offenders
P.O. Box 42018
Washington, DC 20015
(301) 469-6282

Darien Safe Rides
Explorer Post 655
c/o Jane Handley
48 Buttonwood Ln.
Darien, CT 06820
(203) 655-4969

Health Education Foundation
Suite 452
600 New Hampshire Ave. N.W.
Washington, DC 20037
(202) 338-3501

Insurance Information Institute
110 William St.
New York, NY 10038
(800) 221-4954

Metropolitan Life Insurance Co.
Health and Safety Education
   Division
Area 16 UV
One Madison Ave.
New York, NY 10010
(212) 578-5016

Mothers Against Drunk Drivers
Suite 310
669 Airport Freeway
Hurst, TX 76053
(817) 268-MADD

National Association of
   Governors' Highway Safety
   Representatives
Suite 524
444 North Capitol St.
Washington, DC 20001
(202) 624-5877

National Assoc. of Insurance
   Women (International)
P.O. Box 4410
Tulsa, OK 74159
(918) 744-5195

National Assoc. of State
   Alcohol and Drug Abuse
   Directors
Suite 530
444 North Capitol St.
Washington, DC 20001
(202) 783-6868

National Clearinghouse for
   Alcohol Information
U.S. Department of Health &
   Human Services
P.O. Box 2345
Rockville, MD 20852

National Commission Against
   Drunk Driving
1705 DeSales St., N.W.
Washington, DC 20036
(202) 293-2270

National Council on Alcoholism
Suite 1405
733 Third Ave.
New York, NY 10017
(212) 986-4433

National Highway Traffic Safety
   Administration
Office of Alcohol
   Countermeasures
NTS 21
400 Seventh St., S.W.
Washington, DC 20590
(202) 426-9581

The Prevention Center
North Shore Council on
   Alcoholism
183 Newbury St.
Danvers, MA 01923
(617) 777-2664

Remove Intoxicated Drivers
P.O. Box 520
Schenectady, NY 12301
(518) 372-0034

Information Services Center of
  Alcohol Studies
Rutgers University
P.O. Box 969
Piscataway, NJ 08854
(201) 932-4442

Indications of Abuse

COMMON GENERAL SYMPTOMS OF DRUG ABUSE

1. Changes in behavior and character.
2. Sudden loss of interest in normal activities.
3. Lowered grades or poor school attendance.
4. New groups of friends.
5. Unexplained absences of long duration.
6. Poor physical appearance.
7. Wearing sun glasses at unseemly times, concealing red eyes or dilated pupils.
8. Pro-drug reading materials, posters, T-shirts, belt buckles, etc.
9. Coming home from an evening out and going straight to the bedroom.

SIGNS OF DRUG USE AND DRUG EFFECTS

MARIJUANA

1. Greenish-brown dried plant material in plastic bags or small containers.
2. Paraphernalia—rolling papers, pipes, water pipes, roach clips.
3. Small dark seeds, stems, small butts or "roaches."
4. Increased hunger.
5. Excessive reddening of the eyes.
6. Odor of burnt leaves on clothing.
7. Small holes or burns in clothing.

INHALANTS

1. Empty glue or spray cans.
2. Bags or rags with dry paint, glue, etc., in or on them.
3. Dried paint or glue on clothes.
4. Running nose and red eyes.
5. Unpleasant, chemical breath.
6. Increased coughing and salivation.

STIMULANTS

1. Talkative, restless, excited behavior.
2. Excessive perspiration.
3. Tablets or capsules of various shapes and colors.
4. Hypodermic needles, cotton balls, spoons may indicate intravenous drug use.
5. Small packets of a white powdered substance.
6. Mirrors, short straws, single edge razor blades may indicate cocaine use.
7. Chain smoking.
8. Going long periods without sleeping or eating.

DEPRESSANTS

1. User may act as if drunk, with no noticeable smell of alcohol.
2. Slurred speech, staggering, and slowed reactions.
3. Strong body odor on person and clothing.
4. Pills in various shapes and colors.

OPIATES

1. Small packets of powder.
2. Hypodermic syringes, spoons, used for injection.
3. Small spots of blood on shirt sleeves and clothes.
4. Contracted pupils, bruises or scars along veins.
5. Belts or straps used for tourniquets.
6. Users appear very sleepy (nodding), drowsy and lethargic.

HALLUCINOGENS

1. Users sit or recline quietly in a dream or trancelike state.
2. Pupils become very large.
3. While high, a user may "rush" or shudder.

Drug Awareness Test

1. What is the most common reason behind a child trying an illegal substance?
   (a) Curiosity, to see what it's like
   (b) A desire to get high
   (c) Talked into it by friends
2. National statistics show most children have their first encounter with illegal substances at a very early age. The first exposure most often takes place in:
   (a) Fifth grade
   (b) Sixth grade
   (c) Seventh and Eighth grade
3. What is the psychoactive agent responsible for the intoxicating effects of marijuana?
   (a) PCP
   (b) THC
   (c) Cannabinoids
   (d) The resins
4. Opium is derived from:
   (a) A root
   (b) A leaf
   (c) A flower pod
5. Which of the following creates the most severe and dangerous physical addiction, with the added possibility of death during the withdrawal period?
   (a) Heroin
   (b) Morphine
   (c) Barbiturates
   (d) Cocaine
6. PCP, because of its dangerous effects, is often sold on the street as:
   (a) LSD
   (b) THC or Cannabinol
   (c) Psilocybin
   (d) Mescaline
   (e) All of the above

7. Which of the following are directly related to the use of marijuana?
   (a) Loss of memory
   (b) Impairment of the immunity system
   (c) Lung disease
   (d) Amotivational syndrome
   (e) All of the above

8. The most dangerous aspect of injecting drugs directly into the veins is:
   (a) Quick, heavy addiction
   (b) Collapsed veins
   (c) Disease and blood disorders
   (d) High possibility of overdose

9. Which of the following is *not* a true narcotic?
   (a) Opium
   (b) Dilaudid
   (c) Percodan
   (d) Cocaine

10. Which of the following drugs does *not* create physical addiction?
    (a) Barbiturates
    (b) Hallucinogens
    (c) Amphetamines
    (d) They all create addiction

11. PCP was first marketed as:
    (a) A tranquilizer for veterinary use
    (b) An antagonist used for curing narcotic addiction
    (c) A human anesthetic
    (d) Never approved for legal use

ANSWERS:

1. (c) Children named peer pressure, followed by curiosity.
2. (a) The 5th grade, the time when most children will first encounter drugs.
3. (b) THC is believed to be responsible for marijuana's intoxicating effects.
4. (c) Crude opium is gathered from the unripe seedpod of the poppy, *Papaver somniferum.*
5. (c) Barbiturates pose the greatest threat of these drugs. Abrupt withdrawal can be deadly.
6. (e) PCP, considered to be an undesirable drug, often masquerades as other drugs.

7. (e) Studies prove that the use of marijuana can produce harmful side effects—including all of those listed.
8. (c) Through the use of nonsterile equipment and procedures, more drug users die from blood disorders and infectious diseases than from overdoses.
9. (d) The term "narcotic," in its medical meaning, refers to opium and opium derivatives or synthetic substitutes. Cocaine is actually a stimulant with anesthetic properties.
10. (b) Hallucinogens are not physically addicting.
11. (a) PCP became commercially available for use in veterinary medicine in the 1960s.

A SADD Guide to Teenage Parties

For a great party with a happy ending

When your teenager is planning a party:

Plan in advance. Check the party plans with your child and know the guest list. If you agree with the list, you can curb an "open party" situation. Limit the number of guests and let the party be by invitation only. Invitations generated by word-of-mouth bring party crashers.

Set a time limit. Set a definite start and finish; don't let the party go on too long. Consider daytime parties instead of evening ones, or plan alternative activities such as swimming, skating or renting movies.

Agree to the rules ahead of time. These might include:

No drugs, including alcohol
No smoking
No leaving the party and then returning
No gate crashers allowed
The lights should be kept on at all times
Some rooms of the house are off-limits

APPENDIX C

Know your responsibilities. The responsible adult at a teenager's party is visible and *aware*. Remember: *It is illegal to give drugs, including alcohol, to minors.* You may be legally responsible for anything that happens to a minor who has been given drugs or been served alcohol in your home. Most parents are ignorant of the law in this regard; laws may vary from state to state, and you should call your local police department to inquire about your responsibilities. There are criminal charges that can be brought for serving alcohol to minors and for risking injury to minors. Penalties of up to one year in prison, fines ranging up to $1000, or both, may result if a parent is caught allowing minors to consume alcohol.

Alcohol Traffic Safety Education Quiz

Answer True or False to the following questions:

1. One twelve-ounce bottle of beer contains about the same amount of alcohol as a one-ounce glass of whiskey.

2. Alcohol takes longer to be absorbed into the blood system than it takes to leave the body and the brain.

3. A 150-pound person who drinks two ounces of 80 proof liquor during a one-hour period will show a blood alcohol level of approximately .03 percent.

4. In one hour, a 200-pound person can consume more alcohol than a 150-pound person before reaching the same blood alcohol concentration.

5. In the brain, alcohol first depresses the area of higher functions, which includes judgment and reasoning.

6. The effects of alcohol are lessened by eating before or during drinking.

7. The same individual can be affected by alcohol more at one time than another.
8. Alcohol, when mixed with other drugs, can sharply increase impairment effects.
9. Black coffee, cold showers and exercise have considerable influence in speeding recovery from the effects of alcohol.
10. The degree of risk a driver takes is likely to be affected by alcohol before his muscular coordination is impaired.
11. A serious effect of alcohol on a driver is to increase his self-confidence while reducing his ability to act and react physically and mentally.
12. Alcohol is likely to influence the driving performance of young people more than adults.
13. Studies suggest that driving performance does not become impaired until the blood level reaches .10 percent.
14. Approximately half of the drivers killed in highway collisions had a blood alcohol level of .10 percent or greater.
15. A driver with a blood alcohol level of 0.15 percent has a twenty-five times greater chance of causing a highway collision than he would if he were not drinking.

ANSWERS

1. T	9. F
2. F	10. T
3. F	11. T
4. T	12. T
5. T	13. F
6. F	14. T
7. T	15. T
8. T	

Contributors to SADD

State Farm Insurance
Commercial Union Insurance Co.
Miller Brewing Co.
J.M. Foundation
The Commerce Insurance Co.
Harleysville Insurance Co.
General Federation of Women's Clubs
The Oppenheimer Family Foundation
Unigard Insurance Group
Stroh's Brewing Co.
National Coin Machine Institute
National Restaurant Association
United States Brewers Association
Cottey College
Powers & Hall
Government Employee Insurance Co.
Allstate Insurance Co.
Atlantic Companies
Distilled Spirits Council of the United States
Anheuser Busch
East-Pac Corporation
Crum & Forster Corp.
Market Data Retrieval, Inc.
Norton Company
John Hancock Insurance Co.
Joseph E. Seagrams & Sons
Kemper Insurance Co.
L. Knife & Son

APPENDIX E

Lumbermen's Mutual Casualty Co.

Mooney & Company, Inc.

Insurance Information Institute

The George F. & Sybil H. Fuller Foundation

Missouri Valley Federation of Temple Youth

Cape Cod Plymouth & Islands Package Store Association

Honeywell Foundation

J. McGreggor Dodds

National Automobile Association of Dealers

Wine Institute

Seaboard Products

McHenry County Bicycle Club

Mellon Bank

Washington Street Motors

The Rockefeller Foundation

The Stoddard Charitable Trust

Polaroid Foundation

Old Colony Charitable Foundation

Raytheon Co.

Mass. Wholesalers of Malt Beverages

For information concerning programs with Robert Anastas or SADD representatives, SADD films and videos, copies of THE CONTRACT FOR LIFE, junior and senior high school curriculums, school starter kits and SADD custom products, contact:

Students Against Driving Drunk
P.O. Box 800
Marlboro, MA
01752

ABOUT THE AUTHORS

Robert Anastas

Robert Anastas, founder and executive director of Students Against Driving Drunk, has served for twelve years as Director of Health Education for the Wayland Public Schools in Wayland, Massachusetts. During the past twenty-two years, Mr. Anastas has received many distinguished service awards, including the Massachusetts Teacher of the Year Award, an award from the National Commission for the Prevention of Alcohol and Drug Dependency, and the United States Department of Health and Human Services Certificate of Appreciation.

Mr. Anastas is a graduate of American International College in Springfield, Massachusetts, where he earned All-American honors in football and hockey. He received his Master's Degree in Education from Worcester State College.

Kalia Lulow

Kalia Lulow, a freelance writer, has written thirteen nonfiction books, including biographies of Barry Manilow and Julian Lennon; she has also written for television and magazines. She lives in New York City.